D1412886

BOOKS BY BARBARA CROFT

Primary Colors and Other Stories

Necessary Fictions

Moon's Crossing

MOON'S CROSSING

Barbara Croft

A MARINER ORIGINAL

Houghton Mifflin Company

BOSTON   NEW YORK

2003

For information about permission to reproduce selections from
this book, write to Permissions, Houghton Mifflin Company,
215 Park Avenue South, New York, New York 10003.

Visit our Web site: www.houghtonmifflinbooks.com.

LIBRARY OF CONGRESS CATALOGING-IN-PUBLICATION DATA

Croft, Barbara.
Moon's crossing / Barbara Croft.
p.   cm.
ISBN 0-618-34153-6
1. Suicide victims—Fiction. 2. United States—History—Civil War.
1861–1865—Veterans—Fiction. 3. World's Columbian Exposition (1893 : Chicago,
Ill.)—Fiction. 4. Suicide victims—Family relationships—Fiction. 5. Police—New York
(State)—New York—Fiction. 6. New York (N.Y.)—Fiction. 7. Chicago (Ill.)—Fiction.
8. Prostitutes—Fiction. 9. Ferries—Fiction. I. Title.

PS3553.R5367M66 2003
813'.54—dc21   2003047838

Book design by Anne Chalmers
Typeface: Linotype-Hell Electra

PRINTED IN THE UNITED STATES OF AMERICA

QUM 10 9 8 7 6 5 4 3 2 1

The author is grateful for permission to quote from the poem "Seeing the Elephant," originally published in *The Palimpsest*, vol. 30, no. 7 (July 1949), pp. 225–26. Copyright 1949,
State Historical Society of Iowa. Reprinted by permission of the publisher.

For Norm,
who named the book and believed in it from the start

And as to you Life I reckon you are the leavings of many deaths . . .
Walt Whitman, "Song of Myself"

ACKNOWLEDGMENTS

This is a work of fiction. Although actual places, people, and events are mentioned, *Moon's Crossing* is intended to be an impression of an era rather than a historical account.

I'd like to thank the Illinois Arts Council for its support during the final stages of the writing of this book. I also received invaluable support from the faculty and staff at the 2000 Wesleyan University writers' conference and from those at the 1997 and 1998 Humber School for Writers in Etobicoke, Ontario, particularly Tim O'Brien, who has taught me so much about writing. Thanks, too, to the Ragdale Foundation, which offered a quiet haven during the summers of 2000 and 2001. It was in the Blue Room at Ragdale that I worked through final drafts of the book, taking inspiration from Shaw Prairie outside my window. As readers will discover, this surviving bit of virgin tall-grass prairie found its way into the story, both as a setting and as a metaphor. I'm deeply indebted to fellow writers, especially Deborah Cummins, Eileen Favorite, Dan Greenstone, Ellen Slezak, and Lee Strickland, who read and critiqued early drafts of this book and helped me think it through. Particular thanks go to my wonderful agent, Elisabeth Weed, who never gave up on Moon, and to my editor, Heidi Pitlor, whose close reading and good judgment greatly improved the book. I also owe a great debt of thanks to the book's copy editor, Katya Rice.

Descriptions of the World's Columbian Exposition of 1893 are taken from Julian Ralph's *Harper's Chicago and the World's Fair* (New York: Harper & Brothers, 1892). Quotations from the work of

Walt Whitman come from *Complete Poetry and Collected Prose* (New York: Library of America, 1982).

A portion of this book was published as a short story called "The Stone" in *Primary Colors and Other Stories* (Minneapolis: New Rivers Press, 1991). A short version of *Moon's Crossing*, called *Columbia*, was selected by Susan Dodd for a Faulkner Medal, awarded by The Pirate's Alley Faulkner Society, Inc., in 2000. The society's kindness and confidence in my work gave me the courage I needed to finish the book.

Part One

IN AUGUST OF 1914, on the eve of World War I, Jim Moon, then sixty-eight years old, stepped off the stern of a ferry in New York harbor just as the boat passed under the Brooklyn Bridge. A schoolteacher on holiday who happened to witness Moon's exit reported that he was reciting "Song of Myself": *Born here of parents born here from parents the same . . .*

Moon sank like a stone and failed to rise.

"That's impossible," a policeman said.

Nevertheless, it was three days before the body surfaced, a full day more before Jim Moon's remains were identified through the piecing together of random clues discovered in his personal effects. No one knew him except a girl in a hotel room near Second Avenue, the accidental executor of Jim Moon's meager estate.

"He left these," she told the policeman. "Pictures."

The girl produced a sizable stack of drawings, done in chalk on brown parcel paper.

"So, your man was an artist."

The girl shrugged.

They were architectural drawings, crudely rendered. Clearly, whoever had made them lacked the benefits of formal artistic training. Yet, in the sweep of the line, the selection of detail, the bold rendering of negative space, the work showed a certain unmistakable native ability.

"Castles in Spain, he called them," the girl said.

There were also several books, prominent among them a thick green reference work called *Harper's Chicago and the World's Fair,* published by a New York house in 1892. The *Harper's* was badly worn — shattered, a rare-book dealer would say — the pages dog-eared and stained. The boards were loose and held together by a frayed length of faded purple ribbon, and tucked between the pages were a number of yellowed newspaper clippings, along with assorted pamphlets and tracts and a lithograph of a stately, impassive woman, holding aloft a scepter and a globe.

"What's this?" The policeman held up a sketch of a tree stump, rendered precisely to scale on quadrille paper.

"That's his stone."

The weight of Jim Moon's boots and linen trousers pulled him down. For the first few seconds he held his breath. *My respiration and inspiration, the beating of my heart, the passing of blood and air through my lungs . . .*

The policeman studied the sketch of Moon's tombstone. "So, he *intended* to pull a Brodie."

The sunlight faded above Moon's head. The river sealed over him and grew increasingly cold. The turmoil on the docks subsided until he heard only the intimate silence of water. Spiraling down, Moon saw nothing but darkness, saw everything. Drifting, he nudged against a jagged angle of iron and caught. His hair fanned out like a dirty halo. His arms, crooked at the elbow, lifted and fell with the current, moving like wings.

Meanwhile, in Iowa, a burly stonecutter named Hubert Olsen was driving toward a small town south of Winterset with a tombstone in his wagon. Winslow Homer Moon was about to receive his inheritance.

The fact that the stone was delivered on the day of Jim Moon's death was coincidental. Olsen had finished the work that morning and, being eager to collect, decided to close up shop and deliver the stone that afternoon. Stopping to inquire at Varner's dry-goods store—Olsen, of course, was looking for *Jim* Moon—he was directed to Sweetbriar, a second-rate boarding house just north of the square. There he wrestled the stone from the wagon and set it up ceremoniously in the yard.

"I won't accept it," Winslow said. Something about the stone made Win uneasy.

"Where I come from," Olsen told him, "young men shoulder their debts."

Winslow explained that the stone was not his debt, not anything to do with him, but Olsen was determined to collect. He produced a letter that Moon had written him, in effect a purchase order, signed in Moon's own hand, along with a rough design for the stone that Moon himself had sketched on butcher paper.

"He *is* your father," Olsen said, "this James R. Moon?"

Hooked. A jagged scrap of rusty iron had hold of Moon's sleeve. He undulated in purgatorial waters. A brawny gaff man on the surface fished for Moon with a slender pole, swirling the hook in figure eights, but Moon was agile and weightless. He danced away.

"Get a net," somebody hollered. Voices, footsteps. Moon paid no attention. *I am satisfied—I see, dance, laugh . . .* Disaffected, finished now with beginnings and with endings, and not expecting his life to pass before him—not, at least, in any orderly fashion—Moon welcomed instead a crude kaleidoscope of fragments, shards of the old naive totality.

"Almost fifty-five dollars," Mrs. Maythorpe gasped. "How will you ever pay for it, Mr. Moon?"

Mrs. Maythorpe—called Mother by her boarders—was the proprietor of Sweetbriar, where Win Moon had been living since he graduated from high school and took a job with the Reverend Cyrus Rayburn as handyman at the Open Bible Church.

"I simply cannot comprehend," she said, "what in the world your father could have been thinking. A thing like that."

The "thing" was, in fact, a sort of pulpit, three feet eight inches high, carved in cream-colored Iowa limestone to resemble a tree stump, probably oak, twined with ivy. Calla lilies grew at the base, and on the top—this was the part that Winslow found disturbing—lay an open stone book.

"The Book of Life," Pastor Rayburn said, passing Mother Maythorpe's yard and stopping to admire the monument. "Wherein we may read of our sins and our glory."

Winslow had no sins and precious little glory, except perhaps for Caroline, Mrs. Maythorpe's daughter, a stubborn girl of modest looks and impeccable common sense, the perfect mate with whom to live an ordinary life.

"He must of been crazy," Caroline said.

Winslow loved this girl with an ardor that far exceeded her merits and would have married her gladly if only he could resolve certain life questions he had and acquire enough money to win over her practical nature. Their future was compromised, however, by Win's poverty and by the reputation for lunacy Jim Moon had gathered around his family, and now by this unexpected debt, beneath which Winslow squirmed like a bug on a pin.

"Pastor can only pay me sixteen dollars a week," Win said, talking mostly to himself. "And there's my education and my board." Unable to afford the seminary in Des Moines, Win was taking a correspondence course from the Shipley Institute for Self-Improvement in Chicago.

"Well, Mother says you can't leave that thing in the yard," Caroline said. "People talk so."

"I know."

"Mother says people say . . . Well, you know what they say, and they say that your father— Well, Win, he couldn't have loved you very much. Not really."

"I know."

"Or he would have made a home for you, Mother says. That's what people do."

"Caroline, please."

"People don't wander around the world for no good reason and

6

never come home like your father." Caroline was relentless on the subject of Jim Moon. "Well, do they?"

It was late afternoon in Lower Manhattan, and something about the setting sun through the latticework of the bridge—the black and the red—made Moon's final choice seem obvious. He stood up and stretched, a tall man. He drew a last deep breath of harbor air and savored it—fishy, rank, sun-shot, copper-edged—and began to recite. *I celebrate myself and sing myself* . . . When he reached a suitable stopping point, he stepped out of his life.

"A lunatic." Caroline turned her back on the stone.

"And what does that make me, then?" Winslow said.

"The man was a seeker of truth in a timeless text." Pastor Rayburn ran a fingertip down a blank page of Jim Moon's limestone book as though he were in search of a particularly relevant passage. "And no man dares reproach him." He looked at Winslow.

Winslow did reproach his father, however—or at least he tried. Egged on by Caroline, Win nodded sagely whenever old Moon's faults were catalogued. "Well, I guess he *was* sort of eccentric," he said.

"Eccentric?" Caroline affected a wide, theatrical stare. "Eccentric? He was a loony bird. Who else would buy a cement tree stump?"

"It's stone."

"He must have been boiled as an owl, three sheets to the wind."

"Caro*line.*"

"Oh, Win. You know what they say."

In fact, there was some truth to her assertion: Jim Moon had commissioned the stone after a two-day binge of savage drinking. But even if Win had known this fact, he would have tried to deny it. Yes, he was hurt and angry, and yes, he agreed, in theory, that Jim Moon was a sorry excuse for a man. But like most lonely children, Win had learned to comfort himself through imagination, constructing, over the years, a private, blameless make-believe father. This storybook

Moon was handsome, wise, brave, a splendid soldier. He was heroic, of course, but without conceit—a bold horseman, a crackerjack shot. He was an irresistible ladies' man.

Win spent many idle moments filling in the details of this portrait and eluding the factual snares that would have "proven" what Moon really was. This wasn't easy in a small town where "what they say" became, with sufficient repetition, the truth. The facts were hard, what few of them Win knew: that, in October of 1893, Jim Moon, a middle-aged man by then, had left his young wife, Mae—and Winslow, less than three months old—to visit the World's Columbian Exposition in Chicago, and that, for whatever reason, he never came home. Win's mother disappeared the following summer under "mysterious circumstances," and Winslow was taken in by a neighbor lady, Mrs. Ross.

He became "that Moon boy," an isolated, melancholy creature who lived with an invisible mark upon him. Pitied and held in awe by the town as someone whose fate forever remained suspended, Win grew up the same way bread dough swells, out of some ferment inside but without direction. When Mrs. Ross passed on some twenty years later, Winslow Homer Moon was still not "settled."

"Win told Hue Olsen just to take that crazy tombstone right on back," Caroline bragged at supper.

Win blanched. "Caroline, I did not."

"Win's got a level head on his shoulders," Mother Maythorpe said.

Caroline heaped potatoes on her plate and splashed on the thick beef gravy. "Said Jim Moon was no concern of his."

"Well, not in so many words," Win said.

"Integrity," Mother Maythorpe said, beaming at Win. She passed him the succotash. "Some people have it, and some people don't."

"Course, in the end, he had to agree to take it on and pay. That's the law." Caroline hacked at her skirt steak. "But, Mama, you should of seen our Winnie standing up to that man."

In point of fact, Win had done no such thing. As in most confrontations, he had wilted after a brief show of reluctance, and Olsen had bullied him into accepting the stone by scowling deeply and flexing his muscles. Win folded like a paper fan and agreed to pay a dollar a week until the debt was cleared.

It had not been a proud moment. Now, however, hearing Caroline's version of the story, Win reconsidered and seemed to remember that perhaps he had been somewhat decisive.

"Well, it was so unexpected," he said.

Caroline smiled. "I think you done exactly right," she told him. She buttered a slab of bread. "And as for that old stone, why, you know what?" She leaned over and patted his hand. "We're just gonna chop that up into gravel."

The policeman was young and ambitious, a thick, redheaded Irishman with an eye to politics. This waterlogged old codger just could be the ticket. Word on the street was, there was a runner missing, an old man like the stiff in question with the same gray beard and bony physique, supposed to deliver a very interesting bundle from New Jersey to certain higher-ups on the Lower East Side. Only the thing was, the bundle had never arrived.

The policeman glanced at the girl.

"What?"

Naturally, these higher-ups were not pleased. They might be grateful if, in the line of duty, a lowly foot patrolman like himself—helping to identify some poor unfortunate and return his sorry remains to his grieving family—were, by chance, to recover that self-same bundle.

The policeman straddled a wooden chair and draped his arms over the backrest. "So who is this old duffer, anyhow?" he said. "Your da?"

The girl wouldn't answer.

"Don't tell me he's your beau."

The girl stood by the window. Morning sunlight cut across her belly and hips and left her face in shadow.

9

"Of course, we know a bit about him already." The policeman had no qualms about lying if it persuaded the girl to open up. "I'm not at liberty to give you the full details, but . . . His involvement in the rackets, for instance."

"Well, if you know so much, you don't need me."

"I wouldn't say that."

The two of them eyed each other, wary. "It's a complicated business," he said.

She was scrawny, plain, with dirty brown hair that separated into thin, hopeless strands. Nineteen or twenty, sullen, but with a melancholy that the policeman thought he could use.

He stood up and stretched. "You know," he said, trying to scare her, "you just might be implicated here."

Her eyes were red. Her dingy yellow silk wrapper was belted loosely at the waist. Tired, sad. Could a street girl be mourning?

"Accomplice, accessory. People have been known to go to jail for helping other folks do wrong."

This seemed to get to her. "He didn't do no wrong."

The room was hot. The air was close and stuffy. The room was dark, and it didn't help that the walls had been painted a spiritless olive green. The floor was rough oak planking, dull and unpainted, worn by the ebb and flow of hundreds of men. There was a braided oval rug in shades of brown and an old brass wind-up clock on the floor beside the bed.

The girl stepped out of the light. "What's your name?"

The policeman had begun to search the room. "Never mind who I am. It's the old man we're talking about."

The door had been left open to catch what little breeze there was, hiding Moon's old gabardine coat, hung on a wire hook on the back of the door.

"I'd say it's John or Michael." The girl hoped to distract him. "A saint or an angel."

"It's Michael," he said.

"Mike, Mickey, Mick."

"Fine." The policeman was losing his patience. "Now who's this man of yours and where's the money?"

She thought for a moment, weighing her options. "I'm waiting on my lawyer," she told him.

The policeman smiled. He took off his cap and wiped his forehead, grinning, and shook his head. "Sure, that's a good one," he said.

"What?"

"Your lawyer."

"I got friends."

He studied her face, trying to pierce the pale forehead, glimpse the complex engine of her mind, its cunning arrangement of spinning wheels and silver gears. The flash of thought. Probably wondering right now what to tell him and how and how much and in what sequence. Calculating. The girl ticked like a watch.

"I met him in a bar," she said finally. "Dugan's, I think it was."

"And?"

"Nothing but an old man," she said.

The policeman searched through the bureau. He opened the pine wardrobe and peered in. "How old would you say he was?"

"I don't know."

He sorted through her clothing. "Sixty? Seventy?"

"I guess."

He pulled out a blue cotton dress and threw it on the bed, tossed out petticoats and stockings, a tired black hat with a ragged veil. A flurry of underwear followed, men's and women's. "Where's the rest of the old man's gear?"

"You're looking at it," she said.

The policeman checked the shelf above the hanging rod. "He must have had some possessions."

"Just what's there."

The policeman wadded up the clothing and stuffed it back in the wardrobe. "And what way would a man with absolutely no possessions be affording a hotel room?"

"He traveled light."

The policeman thought of Moon's pale face, dripping river water. Was it surprise he had read there, peace, delight, amazement, terror?

"Suicide's the unforgivable sin," he said, musing.

The girl said nothing.

"Flying in the face of God, it is."

She picked up the blue dress and shook it out, hung it back in the wardrobe.

"It's a worse sin than murder," he said. "Worse than fornication. You *know* what fornication is."

"I got a pretty good idea."

Sunlight seeped across the floor, lapping at the legs of the plain wooden table, the two straightback chairs. It gleamed softly on the iron fireplace but left the tossed double bed in shadow.

The policeman wheeled around. "Question," he said. "What's a pretty girl like you doing with a stew bum, and him old enough to be her granddad?"

"Is there some kind of law against old men?"

"Did he give you money?"

"Sure. He was my honey man. Except when he got to drinking."

"Drank, did he?"

"Like a fish."

She sat down on the bed and watched him. "He got sort of balmy sometimes," she said. "Kept reading in this book, this *poetry*."

"So, your man was a poet."

The girl shrugged.

Destroying Jim Moon's tombstone proved more difficult than Caroline had imagined. A crowbar, a hatchet, and a carpenter's hammer all proved ineffectual.

"You need real stonecutter's tools," Win said.

To her credit, she had done some damage: marred the pages of the book a little and chipped off the points of the calla lilies. But at the rate she was going, total destruction was likely to take her a lifetime.

Winslow sat on the porch steps, watching her work on the stone and whittling. "My father only ever sent me one letter," he said.

"That's one too many, I'd say."

"Came all the way from Alaska."

"Win, do you have to do that?" Caroline hated for him to whittle — a total waste of time, in her estimation.

Win folded his bone-handled pocketknife and tucked it back in his pocket. "It said, 'I have named you after a great American painter, and it is my fondest hope that you will live the free and unencumbered life of an artist.'"

Caroline stared at him.

"Well, it *is* a work of art," he said, meaning the stone.

"It is a monstrosity," she said, speaking slowly so as to leave no room for misunderstanding. "And the sooner it is rubble, the sooner we can get on with your life."

The policeman sat down at the table and settled in, stretching his legs out and crossing them at the ankles. "Well, I'm content," he said. He laced his fingers behind his head. "I got all day."

The girl started to pace. "I told you. I met him in a bar. We came back here."

"This is his room, then."

"He was letting me stay."

The old man wasn't carrying any cash when they pulled him out of the water, just the key to this room, but that proved nothing. He probably stashed it first and then stepped off. Lost it, maybe, or he could have been robbed.

Sure. The policeman considered. Some up-and-coming lush-roller might be strolling down Broadway right this very minute with Jersey loot in his pocket. Either that or the girl had it, hidden here in the room.

"Come clean, missy."

"I didn't *know* him," she said.

The policeman raised a cynical eyebrow.

"He wasn't nothing to me."

The policeman's eyes locked in on her. He had a certain way. A liar couldn't stand his gaze.

"Oh, all right," she said.

The girl crossed the room, produced a key from her bosom, and unlocked a dark green carpetbag she pulled out from under the bed.

"He left this." She tossed a worn, leather-bound diary on the table. "He used to read it to me, pages and pages."

"Why don't you read it to me, then."

"I can't read."

The policeman was annoyed. The man had been in the river for two or three days. He needed to be put under, quick, and the boys were getting impatient. This damned girl was making things harder than things had need to be. Besides which, it was murderous hot, a scorcher.

"Girl, I don't believe a word you say."

She gave him a weak, contemptuous smile. "Your beliefs ain't of interest to me."

He picked up the book and examined it. A hundred pages or more in a slanted scrawl, interspersed with drawings—landscapes, portraits. He opened it near the beginning and started to read:

April 22, 1862 – Keokuk
Dear Diary,

The Casualties are coming in from Shiloh. They have turned the Estes House Hotel into a Union Hospital & on account of my age I am to serve there as Orderly. Dr. Hughs—our Surgeon—does five & six Amputations a day with as many buried. We go daily to the Docks for more. Not to hear the cries of the Men, I stuff my ears with cotton wool & hum to myself John Brown's Body and other such tunes.

· · ·

Heat. The sound of flies intent on feeding. The pile of limbs growing in the pit behind the hotel, and Moon with a dirty kerchief tied over his face, swabbing the bloodstained wooden floor of the ward.

"You, boy. Bandit!"

Moon looked up.

An old man lay on an iron bed. "Give me water," he said.

Moon had just turned sixteen when Colonel William Erasmus Deal—Raw Deal—rode into town on a big white horse. Colonel Deal had gold braid on his shoulders. Colonel Deal had a feather in his hat. He had long auburn hair and a trim mustache, and to young Jim Moon, new to manhood, he was a god.

Jim Moon's father had tried to argue with his son. Jim Moon's mother, predictably, cried. But Moon had a boy's vision of smoke and leather, a beautiful, terrible dream, and he was young. He was in love, and nothing could have stopped him.

"Wanting to see the elephant," his father had said, meaning Moon hoped to witness something extraordinary, a marvel. "Home place pretty tame these days, I guess."

It was spring. The scent of water was in the air. Moon's mother sat in the sewing rocker by the window, a tangle of yarn forgotten in her lap. No, no. Light spilled over her shoulders. There was no sound but the clock on the mantel, the wind in the cottonwood trees.

"Well, then, I reckon," the father had said.

Now Moon gave the old man on the bed a drink from a battered tin pitcher.

"'I am poured out like water.'"

"Psalms," Moon said.

"That's right." The old man drank deeply. "'A dry and thirsty land.'"

His eyes were pearly with cataracts. Sweat glistened on his forehead. Beside the bed a jacket hung over a chair. A double row of tarnished brass buttons caught the last of the sun.

"I know what you're thinking," the old man said.

"Sir?"

"Wanting to fight?"

"Yes, sir, I am," Moon said.

The old man coughed up phlegm the color of roofing tar and spit it into a rag. "You're just a boy."

"I'm near nineteen," Moon told him. An obvious lie.

The man smiled and closed his ghostly eyes. "Look around you, son."

Moon scanned the ballroom. Beautiful women in pastel silk had waltzed there under the crystal chandeliers, their plump shoulders bare and white as cream. Moon heard their hoop skirts whispering over the floor.

"What do you see?"

In fact, Moon saw a makeshift hospital ward, beds filled with wounded men. He smelled the stench of death and heard the ceaseless drone of flies. The men, for the most part, were empty-eyed and stared off into nothing. Some were missing arms or legs, and these were the easy cases, it seemed to Moon. Others had wounds so subtle and interior the extent of the damage could not be ascertained.

"See death?"

Moon nodded.

"Despair?"

The old man sat up, leaned on one shaky elbow. "You *see* all that, and yet you're still wanting a transfer."

Moon couldn't explain himself.

"Better give her another think, boy."

"I'd be awful grateful."

The old man cocked his head coyly, peering around the film of the cataracts. "Truly," he said.

Moon nodded.

"Well, I am damned."

Moon joined the Twenty-fourth Infantry, the "Iowa Temperance Regiment," which he described in his diary as made up of men "who touch not, taste not, handle not spirituous or Malt Liquor,

Wine or Cider." He fought well but without conviction, pitying men he should have despised and excusing from his rifle sight those who charmed him in some physical detail—the set of the jaw, a bright bandanna—those who, with some gesture perhaps, reminded him of his own humanity.

Moon was green, with no lust for blood. But sometimes, when a fight was unexpected or the battle turned suddenly and Moon saw the men rush forward, himself among them, throwing their bodies heedlessly into the fray, he felt amazed. He hadn't known he would see that kind of courage, not from the farmboys and storekeepers he soldiered with and thought he knew, and certainly not from himself. To die for your country. Moon was astonished. To give your small, ordinary life for an ideal.

April 26, 1863
Dear Diary,

Camped. Mud to our knees. Seem like she's all Mud from Missouri on down. The Slough of Despond. Most of the boys have the Tennessee Two-Step & no sunlight nor hot food in 2 wks. Sgt. Rourke keeps us cheered. He is as good as they come but old Raw Deal—he rides & we walk & when the Fighting starts up he shows the White Feather. We see him back in the treeline counting the dead.

P.S. Some say they feed these Secesh whiskey & gunpowder to make them fight. I don't exactly believe it but they are hard Boys.

April 30, 1863
Dear Diary,

One of the boys from C company got to fooling this A.M.—pretend to have a Cottonmouth which wasn't nothing more than a Whipsnake. I took him down & talked some sense with my two fist & he seen Reason.

Many Colored on the road. Sons of Ham, Capt. calls them. One old Man with a leg iron hip to ankle bone—a runner—that give his

Gait a sideways amble & we cut him loose of it. Traded looks & give him some Tobac. Brown skin & eyes the color of dried Maple sap. Tried to draw him but dark come on & had to quit.

May 8, 1863 – Hard Times Landing
Dear Diary,
Rains come last night & washed out a ravine nr camp. A Skull come up out of the Mud & it grinning. Some of the boys dug him out & the rib bones danced a swirl. He was busted up but all there & the arm bones were clean & white. Drawed him & got the curves in pretty much right. We think He is one of ours.

May 16, 1863 – Champion Hill
Dear Diary,
At 15 minutes of 8 guns commenced. Weather extremely hot. We come up & fed through other Companies headed for the rear. The Boys held their bloody Hands up for us to see they were no Cowards. Many wounded. At the line there was no advance & we loaded & killed steady for one hour in the Sun.

June 3, 1863 – nr Vicksburg
Dear Diary,
Pushing on. "God defend the Right and bring this unnatural war to a close by the success of our Cause the Salvation of the Union." Amen. Capt. says the people of the South are 100 years behind the North in Enterprise & Improvements & this on account of Slavery.
P.S. I have drawed the Brown Man again but still ain't got him right.

Summer passed. Winter came on—Christmas in the mud—and the year turned. Spring again, summer. Moon fought on. In the fall, Lincoln was reelected over McClellan and the Peace Democrats. The boys in camp whooped and hollered. Winter again.
And then, one chilly day in early spring, near a town that Moon could not have named, he and a boy called Alvin Cobb, caught up in

a running skirmish, became separated from their unit and, without much discussion, decided not to try to rejoin the fighting.

"Let's lay up in them woods," Moon said. It seemed like a good idea at the time.

They turned north and lost themselves in a tangled grove that bordered a shallow river.

"You reckon we're ever gonna win this war?" Cobb said, trudging through the brush.

Moon shrugged.

"They *say* we're winning, the boys."

They came to a clearing and sat down to rest. Moon watched the river slip in and out of the shadows.

Cobb opened his haversack. "She's supposed to be winding down by now."

"Says who?"

Cobb laid out a pouch of tobacco, a long-stemmed clay pipe with a carved bowl. He built a fire and boiled coffee, whistling while he worked. A fair-haired boy from Prairie City, Cobb was slow, but earnest and goodhearted. Moon couldn't help but like him.

"Seem like she's dragging on," Cobb said.

Moon studied Cobb's face: the freckled nose, the jug ears, the muddy, gray-green eyes, flat and expressionless. It was an innocent face, the kind that Moon had noted often seemed marked for death. Moon had seen whole regiments cut down in an afternoon, meadows where the grass was slick with blood, and it seemed to him that the tall, lanky kind, his kind, those who had grown wary and distant over time, were the ones who mostly survived. He watched Cobb and tried to puzzle it out, why some men died and others did not, and whether he himself would die, and, if not, how he could ever go home again.

Moon was no scholar. Politics bored him. What he knew, he knew by intuition, by the feel and sound and smell of things. He carried his diary over his heart, where other boys carried a Bible, and wrote out his thoughts with a stubby yellow carpenter's pencil, using a straightedge to keep the lines from sinking on the right. He recorded the weather, his health and disposition, the birds he spot-ted—warblers, swallows, tanagers—and phonetic reproductions of their songs. On occasion, he soared, pouring out his heart in elabo-rate phrasings when some event had puzzled or angered or moved him, and sometimes he sketched in the margins, trying to capture the lay of the land or the twisted limbs of a burr oak, the curve of the mouth of the old brown man he had seen along the road, his amber eyes. He wrote down the sayings of men he met, recorded their sto-ries. He rhapsodized on women he only imagined, casting them in various roles—companion, wife, a sister he never had.

"Well, we seen the elephant." Cobb held out the tobacco pouch, but Moon shook his head. "Tell true, that old boy ain't all he's bragged up to be."

Cobb drank his coffee. "When she does end, I'm going out west."

Moon nodded. "Sure."

"I'm tired of soldiering," he said.

Moon thought he was joking, but, glancing over, he saw that Cobb's brow was deeply furrowed with unaccustomed thought.

"San Francisco," Cobb said. "Get me a store-bought suit of clothes and a gold-headed walking stick." He finished his coffee and stretched out on the ground. He pulled his cap down over his eyes, and within a minute or two he was sound asleep and breathing easy.

Moon studied him. Tired of war. Cobb's round belly rose and fell. A peaceful snoring came from beneath his cap. Watching him, Moon longed for the same kind of ease.

Tired. Moon started to figure. If he could walk just twenty miles a day, in two months or less he might be home, back in the clapboard house where he was born, the little bedroom with the plain pine walls and the slanted ceiling. Back with his mother, who baked him buttermilk biscuits and patched his jacket and traded off reading out loud with him from a book called *Pilgrim's Progress*. Back with the black-and-white dog he had and the fishing spot on the Cedar River, a steel-gray pool above Columbus Junction. The water there was shadow-laced, overhung with trees, still and timeless, and there, using a string and a crooked threepenny nail, Moon had hooked glossy, mottled bullheads the color of dark winter ice and skinned them out on the bank. Their fat, coiling guts turned the water the color of rusty iron, leaving Moon with the pearl-white fillets going golden over a fire. Moon remembered digging his toes into the cool mud of the riverbank, hungry and waiting for supper, running some scrap of language through his mind: poetry from one of his mother's little leather-bound books, Bunyan or Sir Walter Scott or maybe the Bible, some hymn he had heard filtering out of the white frame Baptist church.

Quietly Moon stood up and gathered his gear. The sun hung low, but it was still possible, he believed, to cover two or three miles or more yet that day. He left the fire burning. He thought about leaving a note but decided against it. Unlike Moon, whose mother had taught him early from the McGuffey, Alvin Cobb probably couldn't read, and anyway he was the kind of boy who told everything he knew.

Moon left him sleeping and walked away. He followed the river, angling northwest, first through a sparse cluster of loblolly pine, then into an open field where the ground was a muddy red clay. A high white plantation rose up in the distance, glowing, fretted with live oak trees, and Moon tried to match that beauty to the wretchedness of the slaves. He thought about the Negroes on the road, headed north like a strong brown river.

A mile or so on, he came to a grove where a brown thrasher, hidden high in the trees, was singing for rain. Perhaps, Moon thought, he should camp. Perhaps he should turn around and go back. He thought about Alvin Cobb and hated him, despised the boyish eagerness that had been his, too, just a few years before. Cobb was tired, maybe, but he'd keep fighting. As for Moon, it was too many for him.

Moon sat down and took out his diary. Lately he had begun to brace his own thoughts with lofty quotations, some copied from books and newspapers and some out of the talk around the fire. "I cannot believe that Providence has allowed this great Nation to flourish," he wrote out in one place, "only to see it destroyed & with it the Hope of millions for Freedom." It was a pretty run of words— Moon liked the way it rolled—but, copied out that way, it lost its force.

To his knowledge, Moon had killed three men—killed in the sense that they were close and he had seen the bewilderment in their eyes: one who appeared suddenly in a woods; one, older, an officer who rushed him on the ridge; and one, a boy about fifteen years old who got in the line of fire. Unanticipated, all three, with no malice intended. Necessary, maybe. Still he mourned. Moon had forgotten their faces, never knew their names, remembered only the strange, twisted postures of their deaths. Cobb was foolish, still a boy, but he was a comrade in arms, and Moon felt some sort of duty to help him stay alive and get that walking stick.

Then, of course, there was the Union.

A slant of light cut through the trees. The sun would set in an hour. Cobb would wake and head on back to the war, and Moon would have to come in alone, finding his way through the dark. He looked north, south again. He was hungry and cold. They would call him a skulker, say he had played off, and, of course, he had. Already he missed the companionship of camp, the men around the fire, the boys he knew, the row of white canvas tents glowing with kerosene lamps, and the murmur of the horses tied along the picket line. To his dismay, Moon had become a soldier.

Moon walked with the sun low on his right, following the river. An hour back, at least, if he wasn't lost. Probably he had already missed supper. And then, how to explain it. Cobb would have some story. *Just got lost, sir,* Moon could hear himself saying.

A girl came out of the woods. She was tall, about Moon's age, and wore a ragged wine-colored dress, muddy at the hem. "Hey," she called out. "You. Stringbean."

Moon was startled out of his reverie.

"Where you headed for, soldier?" She came toward him, smiling. "Looking for me?"

Moon was too tired to speak.

"Ain't lost, are you?"

Moon denied it. "No, ma'am. Tired is all."

She smiled. "I got just the thing."

Moon hesitated.

She reached out and tugged on his ear, teasing. "You can trust me, captain."

Moon followed her into a stand of pines. She sat down and patted the ground beside her. "Come to mama," she said.

Moon glanced over his shoulder. "I'm headed on back to the war," he said.

"It'll wait."

She produced a bottle of bourbon. "That's the thing about wars. They're always there. Miss one, another'll come along."

The girl wasn't dressed for the chilly evening. "You're cold," he said. "I can see the fuzz raised up on your arm." He sat down and put his coat around her.

"Fuzz, fuzz, fuzzy." She liked the word.

"What's your name?"

"Puddin' and tane. Ask me again and I'll tell you the same."

"Tell me."

"You a Quaker?"

"No."

"Talk like one."

"How you mean?"

"I don't know. Kind of sad."

The girl was dark and slender. Moon put his head in her lap and drank in the wild scent of her body. She swept back the fine, curly dark hair from his brow.

"I have a magic elixir hid under my apron," she told him.

"Is that a fact?"

"Uh-huh."

"Give me a taste."

"Find it."

Moon looked up and saw the frank expression in her eyes. "I'm in the Twenty-fourth," he said, "the Iowa Temperance Regiment."

She kissed his mouth.

"Course, I'm not actually with my unit right now."

The girl lay back on the ground and her hair fell loose, spilled out like water. Moon raised himself on one elbow and stared down into her eyes.

She toyed with the buttons on his coat. "Fighting for the coloreds?"

"I don't know." Moon took her hand. "I only ever seen a couple or two before I joined up. And they was a long way off."

"What are you fighting for, then?"

Moon touched her face, ran his hand along the curve of her jaw. "Doing it just to be doing it, I guess."

"Liar."

She rose up and kissed him, brassy. "Got any money?" Her mouth held the smoky taste of the bourbon.

"Nope."

"Well, that's just my luck then, ain't it?"

Moon didn't know what to say.

"Boys," she said.

"I could trade you something."

This intrigued her. "What you got?"

Moon thought for a minute. "Nothing," he said.

The girl fished her hand into Moon's pocket. "Not even a little old two-bit piece?"

Moon giggled. "I'm awful sorry," he said.

She pretended to pout a little, then reached out and ruffled his hair. "Never mind, sweetheart. You ain't the worst I ever seen. Have a drink."

Moon hesitated. Perhaps he knew it wouldn't take much. She kissed him again, and his heart began to float.

"Take it easy now."

She pulled him down between her knees, took a drink, and handed over the bottle.

Moon took a sip, a swallow. Moon drank deep.

"There you go," she said.

The whiskey glowed behind his forehead. Moon closed his eyes, and the weight of the war slipped away. He broke into a smile.

"I told you," she said.

Moon felt light, so easy in his body he seemed to float up over the treetops, and from that vantage point he could see a patchwork of fields in the distance, gentle hills layered in pearl gray. Beyond them, a scatter of woods, the tall-grass prairie, the plains and the mountains, snowcapped, gleaming, giving way on the far side to a valley, incredibly green. Moon saw his way clear to the broad Pacific, which rolled in ancient rhythms, wave on wave.

"What's that you got in them big blue eyes?" the girl said. "Tears?"

Moon slept and dreamed of a long train, draped in black and winding slowly through the towns of mourning. A ghostly steam shrouded the wheels and their throbbing revolutions, and a special car bore a coffin, especially long.

He woke alone. The sky was empty. There was still frost on the limbs of the trees. March or early April. The earth was bare, but, bending down, looking close along the banks of the river, Moon detected the first fine blades of grass.

The policeman threw the diary on the table and stood up. "This is getting us nowhere."

He gathered a few of Moon's drawings, rolled them together, and tucked them under his arm.

"Going somewhere?" the girl said.

"Going and coming back." He pointed his thick index finger. "And I'll expect you to be here."

The policeman slammed the door behind him and walked the length of the hallway, letting his day stick trail along the wall. Flakes of dull yellow paint fell from above the wainscoting and drifted onto the worn carpeting. The stairwell was even hotter than the room, and the only light came from small, high windows at the landings.

The policeman wiped his brow and swabbed the back of his neck. The steps were iron and made a hollow sound as he descended. On the third floor an odor seeped out that he recognized, a mixture of cooked cabbage and baby shit and unwashed bodies. Same as Cherry Street. The stink of despair. *Bought your way out, have you?* This from his younger brother Rowan. A shiny brass patrolman's badge and all the graft that went with it. *Well, Mickey, just don't forget where you came from.*

He had left two more brothers behind, and one of them, Davy, the littlest, wasting away with consumption. A married sister, a mother, widowed young, the old man dying of drink in a needle shop. He and Rowan found the bastard, wet with his own piss, chucked out in an alleyway. "Looks like the rats have give him a nibble," Rowan said. He nudged the body with the toe of his boot.

After that, he was the man of the house. "You're the solid one, Michael," his mother told him. "You're the one we're counting on now."

The policeman reached the first-floor landing, paused, then shoved open the door. "Well, count away."

He crossed the lobby to the desk.

"I'm asking you again. Who belongs to this key?" He dangled it in front of the desk clerk's face.

"Five fourteen. That's the old man."

"Name?"

The desk clerk shrugged. "They come and they go."

"He lived here? Him and the girl?"

"About a month," the clerk said.

"Let's have a look at your register, then."

The desk clerk puffed on a briar pipe. "Don't keep one," he said.

The policeman laid his stick on the desk clerk's shoulder. "Well, now, my boy, that's against the law."

The clerk was a young man, but he had the look of somebody's derelict grandpa. His face was as red as a boiled crab, and his hair was thin and greasy. "Like I'm telling you, they come"—he winked a rheumy eye—"and they go."

The policeman gave up. Work him over later. He rapped his

stick on the counter twice to pound home a little authority and walked away, twirling through the revolving door and into the morning sunlight.

The pavement shimmered with heat. The tops of the buildings seemed to bleach out in a faint, wavering mist. The dog days. The policeman tugged at his collar. Sweat trickled down his back. A priest passed him, a newsboy, a thin woman propelling a heavy black dress. He wanted shade and water. He wanted to rip off his heavy jacket and throw his hat in the gutter, kick off his brogans and be someplace cool and green.

Near the corner a horse was down, a thin, dirty dapple gray, still in harness but too worn out with work and hunger to struggle. The driver was beating him savagely, using the butt of his whip. Blood flowed down the horse's neck and dripped onto the cobblestones. An older woman wearing a gray cotton dress and a hat with an ostrich feather noticed his uniform and started toward him.

"Officer."

He pretended not to hear her.

"Do something," she said.

The crowd surged toward him, all talking at once. "Shoot it, for Christ's sake," somebody said.

He raised his hands, palms outward, began to back away. He shook his head to tell them that he had no time to get involved. Take up the whole damned morning getting it hauled.

He cut across the street, ducking around a dray, and hurried past a Chinese laundry, a lawyer's office, a tannery. An alley opened up, a shortcut. The heat made everything flat and insubstantial. The horse shrieked behind him, and he heard a fight break out, people yelling and kids running, the woman in gray still calling after him.

He ran up the stairs and caught the first train north. The car was crowded: women and crabby children, old men in dark trousers and dingy white linen shirts reading the papers. A hot, gritty wind blew in through the windows. The policeman held on to a leather strap and swayed like a hanged man.

.   .   .

Back at the hotel, the girl carried a china pitcher down the hall to the bathroom for water and rattled the door handle.

"Occupied!"

The voice from beyond the door was one she knew. "Get out, Stashovick," she said, "and take your stink with you."

"Occupied."

She paced the hall, placing her slippers precisely in the curve of the carpet's overblown cabbage roses. Was that the kind of man a girl could marry? A dumb mick with the heft of boiled potatoes on his breath? Hell of a price to pay, but it was one way out, and—look on the bright side—the man could always die in the line of duty. Somebody with a derringer, a knife. Might leave a little something, and after a bit of play-acting—*Oh, my beloved* . . . What the hell was his name again? Gone forever!—a girl could get herself a little flat and fix it up nice.

She pounded on the bathroom door.

"Can't a man even take a crap in peace?"

She balanced the pitcher on her head, steadying it with her left hand like the woman in one of the pictures Moon had shown her. A Street in Cairo. The women there wore silk trousers and short jackets and did the *dans de ventre*, the belly dance. She walked the length of the hallway. The posture lifted her breasts and forced her to hold her head up high, persuaded her narrow hips into a sway. The *dans de ventre*, the Midway Plaisance. Moon had told her the world was beautiful once.

She turned at the stairwell and walked back, dropped the pitcher to her side, and pounded on the bathroom door again.

"Occupied, I'm telling ya."

The car emptied out a few blocks north, and the policeman found a seat from which he could peer into the windows of passing tenements. Glimpses only they were, like the flip-books, the stereopticon views: a girl at the stove, a woman sewing, a boy coming up the back stairs with a growler, an old man sick or asleep in his iron bed. The way they passed in measured order calmed him down a bit.

Horses. A kind of forgiveness in their eyes. Horses everywhere then, not like now. The other boys tormented them, mean little buggers, throwing stones, worse, but never himself. Waiting mornings for the iceman and begging chips from the wagon, the scent of straw and leather and good honest horse manure. A bay with a thin white blaze, he remembered. A little calf-kneed and long in the tooth, but what an old darling she was.

And Dad was mostly sober then. Mother, still young. His older sister, Lily, was slender and not a bit forward like some of the girls, her skin so white the blue of her veins showed through. Her with the long red hair, getting married to the big butcher, Kegan, who had a nice little shop of his own, and he, Sean Michael, wearing a new wool suit.

The policeman stood up and waited for his stop.

Black as a crow it was, he remembered, with long pants, like the suit of a grown-up man. Himself, the oldest of the boys, with a fresh white chrysanthemum in his lapel.

She'd be damned if she'd give the old man up, and as for the money, well, finder's keepers. Moon had it last, and wasn't she sort of his heir? She looked around her—the faded carpet, the flat wash of dingy sunlight staining the walls. She doubled her fist and pounded on the door.

"Still occupied," the voice said calmly. "These things take time."

Once upon a . . . Gone before she was born. Burned to the ground, the fabulous White City. Music and light forgotten, magic—if it ever existed. Only Moon seemed now to remember. Told her stories alone in the room at night. So detailed she could almost see the buildings, looped like a string of pearls, the blue lagoon.

The policeman got off the train north of the park and walked west to Columbia. He entered the first building he came to and asked the first woman he saw sitting behind a desk.

"I'm afraid I don't understand," she said.

"I'd like a word with one of your professors. Someone who's a genuine expert on art."

"What kind of art?"

"Art."

"Pre-Columbian, medieval, Renaissance?"

"Do you see this badge now?"

"I could hardly not."

"I expect cooperation," he said.

The woman stifled a smile. "Why don't I call someone?"

The man who eventually came forward was a Dr. Christian Fowler, a specialist in antiquities. He ushered the policeman down the hall and showed him into his office, a quiet, cool, oak-paneled room with Gothic windows that looked out over a leafy courtyard.

"I've come about these," the policeman said. He spread the sketches on the desk.

"Please." Fowler swept his arm toward a large leather armchair.

"Thanks, no. Now, this is the way of it . . ."

Fowler raised his hand. "If you'll just allow me."

The professor rubbed the corner of a drawing between his fingers and thumb. "Not old," he said. "Twenty, twenty-five years, judging by the paper. Not quality paper. See how it's foxed here, along the edge?"

The policeman nodded uncertainly.

Fowler produced a magnifying glass and examined the drawings more closely. "Nothing of exceptional artistic merit, of course."

"Did I say they were?"

Fowler stopped and looked up. Again he motioned toward the leather chair. It did look inviting. "Please," he said. "I insist."

The policeman sat down and closed his eyes. The leather was butter soft, and the chair seemed to fit him just right. So this was another world, then, a slower world. This was a place where a fellow could take his time. He drew in the cool, dank quiet of the room and the tension seemed to drain out of him. A faint breeze from the open window lifted his hair. Somewhere in the darkness he heard the comforting tick of a Regulator clock.

"Perspective is a sophistication of art," Fowler said, launching into a lecture, "a disengagement, a letting go. The child, rendering, not what he sees, but what he knows is there, draws a flat rectangle like this"—he sketched in the air—"and calls it a house. In this way, paradoxically, his 'real' world is an emblem."

"Sure," the policeman said, drowsing.

"The artist here, for example"—he tapped one of Moon's drawings—"needs to be *taught* to see. To duplicate, not the idea, which is rectangular, but a narrowing wedge, a disappearing building. For, in our vision, everything moves away."

The policeman had stopped listening. *Moves away, moves away.* Horses, dapples and roans, shot through with sunlight, almost transparent, ghostly, they were so strongly illuminated. And he himself in a field among them. Blue above, incredible light. Grass and shifting treetops. Space. A tender, watery green that seemed to breathe.

"This man had no training, no 'art,'" Fowler said, musing. He shuffled through Moon's sketches. "As *drawings*, they're totally worthless."

He sorted through them again, peering closely. "I must say, however, they do have a certain . . . ardor."

The policeman's eyes flipped open.

"They're raw, of course," Fowler went on, "untutored. But look at the eagerness here in the line."

The policeman leaned forward, looked, looked again and saw nothing.

"A reverence," the professor said. "Here was a man in love."

The quiet that filled the room became oppressive. The clock became insistent. The heat of the policeman's body had warmed the leather chair, which began to cling. Peace was temporary, he learned, as if he didn't know it, and heat and frustration were the order of the day.

Fowler cleared his throat. "But, of course, that's not why you've come." He bundled up the drawings and handed them back.

"What are they pictures *of*, is what I need to know."

"There's only one I recognize."

"Brooklyn Bridge," the policeman said.

"Exactly." The professor held it up. "A pretty fair sketch, too."

"What about the others?"

"Well," Fowler said, "clearly, they're buildings."

"Jesus, Mary, and Joseph, man, don't I know that?"

"You want me to tell you where, when." Fowler took the drawings back and leafed through them again. He selected one at random and dropped it on the desk. "Judging from various architectural details . . ." He shuffled a second drawing to the top of the pile, then another and another, and, illustrating his thought with a thin sterling pointer, pronounced the buildings, in turn, neoclassical, Romanesque, Italian Renaissance, and Greek-Ionic.

"So this is a world traveler, then," the policeman said.

Fowler rolled up the drawings and handed them back. "Possibly."

Winslow stood up and stretched his bones. "Suppose this means he's dead?"

"Who?" Caroline was abusing the stone.

"My father."

"Oh, him."

"I think if he was, I'd know about it," Win said. "Sense it, you know? Or they'd send him home. After all, he *was* a veteran."

Caroline switched from the hammer back to the crowbar.

"He lost an eye," Win said.

"That seems pretty careless."

"In the service of the Union."

Win imagined his father charging into battle, the white smoke of cannon fire drifting over his head. His uniform was the purpled blue of twilight—and not a stain upon it. He wore a forage cap pulled low on his brow, a fringed yellow sash. Moon carried the regimental flag—no. Win changed his mind. Moon was helping a wounded comrade from the field when, suddenly—and this was always the saddest, the most glorious moment—a single ball detached itself from all the others whizzing through the air, and, moving with intention, sought Moon out. It grazed his cheek, the rim of the eyelid, going deep. Cruel lead. It pierced the cornea, the sky-blue iris.

Moon fell to his knees. This was late in the war, one of the last scattered battles—Win wasn't sure which one. Moon refused assistance and kept on fighting. Later, in a makeshift hospital tent, a field surgeon stitched together the mutilated flesh, leaving the eye in an angry, puckered wink.

"'You should ought to go home,'" Win said. "That's what the rest of the boys told him."

"Did he?"

"Nope. Tied a red bandanna over his eye and kept on fighting. Later he made a patch out of scrap leather."

Caroline was exhausted. She sat down on the porch steps and wiped the sweat from her brow. "A sledgehammer. That's what we need."

"He was a hero."

"I think the blacksmith has one."

"Never gave up. My father believed in the Union."

Caroline cupped her hand around Win's ear and leaned in close. "I *said*, I think the *blacksmith* has one."

The war had changed everything. Not obviously at first, but the ground had shifted. Industry had taken hold, bending men to its needs. Farming had changed. Steam power, boom times. A lot of the boys were drifting toward the cities. Money was easy got, Moon heard. Speculation and graft. Fortunes, made in steel, oil, grain futures, railroads, and real estate, concentrated in the hands of a few clever men.

And yet the dead were all around, their daguerreotypes on the parlor tables, their statues in the parks. They haunted memory, and those who had lived and returned, like Moon himself, with empty sleeves, some, with hollow eyes, like ancient mariners, cast a gloom, unsettling social gatherings with their stories.

Already, home for less than a week, Moon had worn out his welcome and begun to annoy the townspeople with his comments. The village he knew as a boy, once the source of numerous possibilities, struck him now as cramped and backward, the girls a little too eager. The river was narrow, not as deep as he remembered it, sluggish and curdled with silt, and the pond where he used to skate on winter afternoons, the sun so bright on the ice that the glare was like lightning, seemed to him now hopelessly small, a playground for children. How had he ever amused himself there? Why, a fellow would just be getting his speed up good, sailing along, when he would have to turn back sharp at the bank. The stores offered nothing that Moon wanted. The bell of the Baptist church had a hollow sound.

"Don't you know men have died?" Moon said one Sunday morning at services—the preacher was deep in some abstract notion of grace. Just stood up and faced the congregation and said it.

The men coughed and shuffled their feet. The women, with their faces blank, turned their heads demurely to look at him. The brims of their stiff black bonnets narrowed their vision, just like the blinders that horses wear.

"And 'died' doesn't even begin to say it." The boys were blown apart, cut down, crushed beneath the wheels of the caissons, caught in ground fires and burned alive—so many horrors Moon couldn't tell it true. He turned away. A colored boy about Moon's own age sat in the back row, watching.

After services Moon wandered out on the prairie. It was June. The fat, humid days were coming on, the coneflowers swarming with skippers. Oxeye and prairie phlox bloomed, the strange, twisting porcupine grass. Milkweed and Turk's cap. Abundance. Once, the old-timers said, the summer grasses grew so tall a traveler could lose sight of Lone Tree or Pilot Mound or whatever landmark he had been aiming for. A sea of grass. It flowered in waves, first the wood sorrel and star grass, low to the ground, pasqueflower, the first to bloom, warming the earth by catching the wind in the tiny hairs of its leaves. Each species struggled upward, flowered in its time, seducing insects with its shrewdly patterned nectar guide, inviting a swarm of procreation, after which the flowers fell back, spent, fragmented to seed, the roots alive, and other plants came on, taller, stronger—gayfeather, false indigo.

At Moon's feet a bull snake parted the grass. The wheat was in, potatoes and Indian corn, a good crop, if there was rain, a good season, but Moon was looking west. Beyond the southern drift plain the loess hills rose up along the Missouri, angular and deeply shadowed. Farther on, the shallow, meandering Platte and the Niobrara, the sand hills and the high plains, the mountains.

"I can't stay," Moon said that night over supper.

Moon's father nodded.

"I just feel like I'm simmering inside."

Moon's mother stood up and cleared the table. Moon couldn't tell if she was grieving or angry with him or what. How many times, he wondered, had he noted that precise part in her hair, the set of her shoulders—all of her mannerisms unspeakably dear. He could draw the lines of her small, oval face by heart, the cameo brooch she wore, the white lace collar.

"There's pie," she said quietly, "if anybody wants."

Through the night mosquitoes teased at the screen. Moon's legs ached. He couldn't sleep. A yellow moon hung low in the sky. Moon got up and lit the lamp to wash away its brightness.

The morning dawned pale and hazy, hot, and even early, the grass was limp with the heat and the horses dozed in their stalls. Moon helped with chores for the last time—milking, drawing water—and ate his breakfast: fried cornmeal mush with maple syrup, scrambled eggs and ham and toasted bread with apple butter. He drank an extra cup of sweet black coffee, mostly for his mother's sake.

"Well." Moon stood up. His carpetbag was packed.

His father pressed some money into Moon's hand. His mother had packed him a lunch of bread and summer sausage and blueberry cobbler. She tucked in a jar of cold coffee. "That's all I can think to do," she said. She started to cry and stopped herself.

"No, that's good," Moon told her. "That'll be good."

. . .

Back in the room the girl poured the water into a tin basin, stripped to the waist, and washed her face and neck and armpits. She parted her yellow silk wrapper and took a swipe at her crotch. She brushed her hair a hundred strokes and changed into the blue cotton dress.

Some people didn't want to be found, ramblers, and as for the money, some people didn't care. Like Jim Moon. After all, he paid her for doing nothing. She pictured him at the table, the dull glow of a single electric bulb overhead sculpting the hollows of his face. He has his head cocked, using the one good eye, reading from a red leather book, the book he refuses to read to her and keeps in the battered footlocker under the bed. "What you don't know won't harm you," Moon likes to say.

He is an old man, thin, his hair wispy as frayed wire. She watches him from the bed. The Half Moon. She's been with him almost a year now, and that craggy profile and hunched back have become familiar to her, dear.

"What time is it?" she says.

He looks up. "Time you slept." The Full Moon, his face toward her, the smile, the gentle way he looks at her, almost like a father.

He closes the book, stands, a thin silhouette, and crosses the floor. He climbs in bed, careful not to brush against her.

The pillow sighs. The springs complain.

"And you," she says.

Moon's bones, sharp at the hip and knee and elbow, Moon's whiskers on the counterpane. He folds his hands outside the coverlet. "What about me?"

"You need some shut-eye, too."

He stretches out his long, thin legs, and the twisted, horny-nailed big toe of his right foot finds a tiny tear in the sheet to worry. "Know what made the soil so black? Rich?"

It's only Moon in one of his rambles.

"Death," he bellows. "The joe pye and rosinweed, the goldenrod, it all dies back. Sinks down and rots away, but it survives. Do you know why?"

She shakes her head.

"Taproots. Snaking down. Ten, twenty feet sometimes. So deep even fire can't kill them out."

"Keep your voice down, Moon."

"They flower again. It all returns." He rears up and glares at her. "Did you think it ended, ever?"

"Moon."

"It only seems."

He sinks back and is silent for a while, breathing evenly, his face impassive. She thinks he is finally asleep.

"Roots," he hollers. "Roots of oaks and hickory. Live for a hundred years or more. And if your plow's in good trim, then it'll cut right through. Turn over roots like winter turnips, slick as a schoolmarm's elbow, but if not . . ." His good eye glistens. "Girl, do you know what happens then?"

"Moon, I don't give a damn."

"Why, the roots will heave that plow of yours right up out of the ground. The earth will spit you out."

They stare at the ceiling, which is so dark it might not even be there. They could be looking up at the infinite black roof of the world.

"Tell me about her," she says.

Moon turns away.

"Moon."

"Water under the bridge."

"I know she's in there," the girl says. "In that book."

Moon says nothing.

"What was she like?"

Moon sighs. "Innocent. Blameless. Eyes the color of prairie gentian."

"Was she pretty?"

Moon sobs, sudden, loud, covers his mouth with both hands. His good eye swims in tears.

"Hey, hey." She places a feather pillow under his head. She strokes his hair. "Settle down, old man."

.   .   .

Moon went west. Memories of the men and boys he had known in the war went with him. He carried the comfort of his mother's voice, his father's stock wisdom. He traveled light. Moon made it all the way to California and stood at the end of his possibilities, nothing much in his pocket but a stubby carpenter's pencil, salty sea waves licking his worn-out boots.

Remembering Moon, the girl started to cry. She hadn't expected that, so maybe she cared. Yeah, a little and didn't know it. Loved him. So trading his stuff for some advantage wasn't like selling him out. She wiped her tears on the back of her hands. Besides, old Moon knew all about betrayal.

Moon's overcoat still hung from the hook on the back of the door. She rummaged through the pockets and found the money in loose bills — Moon must have opened the bundle and taken a dollar or two for drinks. A note was attached in Moon's hand, and though most of it was just squiggles, she recognized her name: four hunched shapes like twisted black wire, the right one dipping down, the left like a camel, like Brooklyn Bridge, Moon said, trying to teach her to read. *Mary*. He meant it for her.

"Moon, Moon," she murmured. In over his head.

Moon wandered. Only the land was constant — mountains, bayous, remnants of tall-grass prairie, eaten away, more and more, by farms, fenced and scarred by roads, but still, it seemed to Moon, indomitable. Untouched or under cultivation, the prairie moved him. Acre on acre, swell and swale, rolling with grasses of bittersweet green in summer, tarnished to a dusty beige in the fall. But living, always alive, with wild lupine and alumroot, bellflower, valerian. Inexhaustible.

And fed by fire.

Moon saw it first in western Nebraska. He had hired on with a local rancher, bucking hay, and the crew had stopped for water. Moon had the dipper to his lips when he looked up and saw a huge black cloud roiling against the sky.

"Stay put, boys," Porter said, the boss. "You'll never outrun it."

A thin line of flame raced along the horizon. Dust flew in the wind. The horses shuddered and danced on the chaff, and their eyes rolled in terror. Porter, who had been driving the wagon, unhitched the tug line and wadded the reins in his hand, jumped on the back of the near horse to hold them.

The fire had created a windstorm, sucking up air and dry grass, driving itself along. A shapechanger. Indians called these sweeping fires the red buffalo. Mostly it moved low to the ground, but now and then a burst of flame would rear and leap forward, a pillar of fire.

There was a good-sized field nearby, fallow, recently harrowed. "Let's move over there," Porter said. He gave the horse a nudge with his heel. But one of the men panicked. He turned and ran, cutting diagonally toward the horizon. Porter yelled, but the man kept right on running.

"God damn it," Porter said. The shape of the man's pale shirt grew smaller, struggling in the smoke. It started to fade.

"Turn back!" Porter yelled.

Near the horizon, the shape of the man disappeared.

Fear swept through the crew. They turned and ran, Moon along with the rest. His long, skinny legs pumping, he reached the safe ground just as the fire shifted.

Moon whirled around. The heat came first, sweeping over them, a furious draft. No air, no sound. Moon and the others were caught in a curious still point, a moment of calm that stretched thin, gathering force. Then the fire rose up. It circled the edge of the field, chattering. The men stood their ground. The heat was intense. Moon had never seen this kind of devastation before, but he knew the sound, like the flow of a river, laughter, empty boxcars clicking over the ties.

The flames billowed, subsided, like breathing, teased along the edge of the field and receded.

"That's it," Porter said. "It's passed on."

The men smiled, took off their hats and wiped their brows. It was over. They all began to talk at once, but Moon turned his back on their babble and walked away.

His lungs were full of smoke, and every bone in his body ached. The sun was going down, disinterested; the earth was still turning. At the edge of the hayfield, he stopped. The wagon was rolling slowly, still in flames. Fire swept out like wings from the spokes of the wheels. Moon, dazzled, spellbound, oddly sleepy, hunkered down. He pulled up a blackened stem and found that the roots were fleshy, alive.

The girl glanced around the room. Not the bureau, not the carpet-bag—too obvious. If and when he came back, the mick would paw through everything. Under the rug, then, in the flue. No. There. Perfect. Tuck it away, a bill or two at a time, in between the pages. The last place the cop would be likely to look.

She found a scarlet ribbon and tied it around her neck. Jewelry was long gone, even the star-shaped garnet pin, pawned for a drink or two, and better that way, Moon had told her, because the star was un-lucky.

She had protested, arguing on the street. *It's all I've got that be-longed to my mother.* Moon pried it out of her hand.

The girl heard the policeman on the stairs, his heavy brogans, the day stick clicking along the balusters. She heard him stop to rest on the fourth-floor landing. Too much brisket and beer. He climbed again: a step and a rest, a step and a rest.

She twisted her hair and piled it on top of her head, then took it down and rearranged it into a modest chignon bunched at the nape of her neck. She studied herself in the mirror, turning her face to the left and then to the right. The chignon was less flippant, more se-date, the kind of look that would keep the policeman guessing. She'd gotten off on the wrong foot with the man, but there was no use burning bridges. She pinched her cheeks to give them a rosy color.

Sure, win him back. Tell him stories. Keep him there and dole it out a little bit at a time. Wait. Wait, at least until she knew the name of the game. With Moon gone, there was nobody she could trust.

Flirt a little and see where it went. Old Mr. Moon wouldn't mind. Could be some kind of reward. If the cop could be trusted, she might just show him the devil's book and get him to read a bit. Find out who her mother was, once and for all.

The sledgehammer proved effective against the stone, but Caroline lacked the strength to lift it more than three or four times, and Win refused to participate in the destruction. Consequently, the only damage done was a sizable crater she had managed to bash in the base of the limestone pulpit and another one dead center in the Book of Life.

"Sweetheart," Win said cautiously, "why don't you take a rest."

Caroline wiped her brow and leaned her hammer against the stone. "I am kind of wore out," she said.

They sat on the back porch steps and watched the sun go down over Mother Maythorpe's garden. The tomato vines were heavy with fruit. The sweet corn was coming on.

"Pastor Rayburn thinks I should set up my father's stone in the churchyard," Winslow said.

"At the Open Bible?"

Win nodded. "He says I got a pulpit, I might as well be a preacher."

Win picked up a stick and began to whittle. "I don't know what I'd say, though."

Caroline sighed. "Well, that ought to tell you something. You *are* just about as silent as the tomb." She leaned over and kissed his cheek. "I don't mean that mean."

Sometimes, when no one was looking, Win drifted away from his work—stacking the hymnals, cutting the grass in the church-yard—and took the pastor's place behind the pulpit. There, looking out over the dimly lit sanctuary, he preached, silently, to a small but enraptured imaginary flock. His text was always the same—sin and redemption, the great eternal core of love and art—and though he knew next to nothing about either subject, his invisible congregation would gaze up from the pews in admiration.

"Pastor says for me just to tell the truth," Win said.

"That's sensible."

"Pastor says, 'A word to the wise is sufficient.'"

Moon tried homesteading, gold mining. He worked as a gandy dancer for the railroad. And every place he went he saw a shadowy piece of the old vision, but never again the vision whole and solid. He joined a threshing crew, hard work from dawn to dusk and broken only by dinnertime, which was fried chicken and biscuits and gravy and string beans and hominy and bread-and-butter pickles and ripe tomatoes and apple pie—Moon liked pie—and cups of strong, hot coffee with lots of sugar. He was still young then—twenty-eight, twenty-nine. The men ate outside at a long deal table in a grove of cottonwood trees, shoveling in the food and flirting hopelessly with the shy Bohemian hired girls.

Moon became a store clerk, which he didn't much like, a teamster, which he did. He understood horses, knew their restlessness and their will. Moon was in his prime then, tan, strong as a bull calf, in the pursuit of happiness, he said, if anyone ever asked his business.

Miraculously, he fell in love, or thought he had, and quit drinking for a month or so. This was in Kansas, and Moon was thirty-four. She was a dressmaker, pretty but prim, better educated than he was, sharp and sure of herself. Moon tried to meet her expectations. But after a summer of courting in the parlor, the girl left him for a young minister.

Moon drifted, followed the Mississippi down to New Orleans, glided east. The proud new Athens, for which the rebel boys had given their lives, was gone, but Moon still saw the ghost of it everywhere, like the ring a glass of whiskey leaves on a table.

He headed west again, and the land sustained him. The sumac going ruby red along the right-of-ways, the splashes of purple among the grasses, the bitter lemon yellow, the sift of white. The way the sun washed over a meadow, mornings. The smell of clover, the sweet-grass smell.

Caroline didn't have much patience for preaching. Imitation pearls before genuine swine. But for Win the stone had suggested possibilities.

"Pastor's right. It's a pulpit," he said.

"It's a *tombstone*."

"On the surface."

"That's what I'm talking about."

Caroline stood up and went inside to start supper.

"That stone's a message," Win said, trailing after her. "A kind of a dare. My father's trying to tell me something."

In the kitchen she tied on a white cotton apron and stoked up the stove. "Supper in forty minutes," she said. "You want biscuits or corn dodgers?"

"I don't care," he said.

"Well, don't sulk."

Win sat down at the kitchen table and took an apple from the fruit bowl. "I think I *am* fixing to set that stone up down in the churchyard," he said.

Caroline glanced up from the stove. "No, you are not neither."

"Oh, but I am." Win's enthusiasm lifted him to his feet. "And I'm going to preach, too. Every Sunday, right after regular services."

"Win," she said, "people don't want to be sermonized all day long. Besides, what training have you had? Other than going to all those boring Chautauquas?"

"Pastor says to listen to my heart. And tell the truth, he says. That's the main thing. And anyhow, I know something about—"

"What? Being a crazy man's son?"

Caroline measured two cups of flour and dumped them into a bowl. "You ought to forget about that old loony."

"Now, wait just a minute."

"Win, he never came *home*." She added a pinch of salt, two level teaspoons of baking powder. "Just kept right on keeping on. Reach me the milk."

She cut in some lard and added a scant cup of buttermilk. "He ended up in New York City," she said. She punished the dough with a wooden spoon. "I rest my case."

Moon was a pick-and-shovel man, a cook, a lumberjack; he was a bargeman on the rivers; he was a tramp. There were other women, less particular. Moon compared them all to an ideal beauty in his mind and found them wanting. He began to stoop a little, took up smoking, let his hair grow long. A wry sort of melancholy set in. Mostly it was impatience, longing that had festered like a wound. Hard work could usually hold it at bay.

He read a lot, knew things now—politics, history, art. His writing improved, his drawing. But he could still be fooled by a clever man or a pretty girl. He still wanted something he couldn't define. In the daylight, in the world of work, the purpose of his life seemed clear. But at night, riding the freight cars, walking the roads, the horror of the war and the vision he had of America often combined in curious patterns, and Moon couldn't tell whether he was chased, driven, or led.

And then in the fall of 1892 Moon was passing back through Iowa and met Miss Mae Eliza Stanton Greentree, who owned a house of sorts and a scruffy farm her father had left her. She was twenty-five years old, and Moon was forty-six.

The policeman had lifted an apple for the girl from a fruitmonger and sat on the bed in the hotel, watching her eat.

"I wasn't sure you'd come back," she said.

She'd fixed her hair while he was gone, put on a little powder. "Maybe I enjoy your company."

Her lips curled back, revealing small, dingy teeth, the canines very sharp and perfectly shaped.

"Tell me the truth about this old man."

The girl seemed more relaxed. "He come from Iowa," she told him. "I don't know the town."

The policeman rummaged through the carpetbag. "Leave any valuables?"

"Huh?"

"Money, jewelry, stocks and bonds?"

"Ha!"

The Greentree place was a sod house, hunched against the wind. Originally there were two small rooms tunneled into a hillside, a sod roof supported by eight thick stripped cottonwood beams. But over the years oddly shaped rooms had been added—a second, a third bedroom, a harness room, a lean-to summer kitchen, slapped together with rough pine—so that by the time Jim Moon arrived, the house spread out from the hill like a maze. Moon and Mae were married in what she liked to call the parlor on a chilly Sunday afternoon with only the preacher from town and a neighbor lady, Mrs. Ross, and her husband, Henry, in attendance. The ceremony was brief but binding. Afterwards, to celebrate, Ross uncorked a large, dubious jug of homemade cider.

November 2, 1892

Dear Diary,

Cold Water seeping in through the Walls. Rain ever day. They say early frost. I don't sleep good—Dreams come at me. Money troubles. Mae. Out in the Feedlot we sink to our knees & cannot leave the house but the Earth wants to suck us down. Hands stiff with the Rheumatism & no relief but the Bottle.

I despair of making a go of farming & my Wife is away too good for me I fear. So young. I have waited too long perhaps & have taken on too many burrs.

Meanwhile I read in a book of Mr. Whitman's Poems which was give to me by a Woman over Town & am strongly moved.

. . .

Win finished the apple and tossed the core in the garbage bin. She was probably right about the preaching. What would he say? The truth was, he was sort of bashful and not much good at anything but sketching—portraits, landscapes, still lifes. What good was that? A man couldn't keep a wife by drawing pictures. His stepmother, Mrs. Ross, had been the town's grade-school teacher for seventeen years, and spent the bulk of her class time going over the three R's. On Saturday mornings, however, she gave drawing lessons at home to the local girls and served them tea in china teacups to help them work on their manners. When Win was ten years old, he joined the class.

She taught him how to shade the charcoal with his fingers, how to use the loose swing of his arm to pursue the line. His early efforts were promising. Win had an eye for texture and composition, but somehow he could never get the hang of seeing things round, sensing their depth and heft so that they came alive on the page. Watching Caroline bustle around the kitchen, he felt like he might want to pick up a pencil and try the thing again.

She was tall and sturdily built, with hair the color of new rope and big mudduckle eyes. If he were to sketch her now, up to her elbows in flour, he would want to catch the angle of her collarbone, the curve of her hips. She had her sleeves rolled up. The ribbon she used to tie back her hair had come loose. Win liked her best this way, disheveled. Even her iron will seemed slack at such times, malleable. He stood up and put his arms around her waist.

"Win, quit it. Mama's right in the parlor."

She pushed him away, but he came right back.

"I don't care," he said.

"You're awful brash."

The girl traced a figure eight on the tabletop, moving her finger in slow curves. "And just who's this 'woman over town' is what I'd like to know."

"Maybe a whore like yourself," the policeman said.

"Well, what if she was? Look, if you ain't taking me in, then don't offer me no sermons."

"I'm sorry," he said. His own sincerity surprised him. "Truly. I'm a bit rough sometimes."

He sat down at the table and studied the girl. "And, anyhow, what way would I be in the sermon business?" he said. "Sure, you know there's no money in that."

He pulled a white handkerchief out of his pocket and mopped his brow. "All I say is, a stray dog like this old geezer doesn't deserve the love of a good woman."

"Ain't none of you do."

Mae Moon lit the lamp and set it on the little round parlor table. She was fair, with hair the color of clover honey, a little too tall for a girl—that was her opinion. Her eyes, most people thought, were her best feature, round and wide-set, the color of prairie gentian, but Moon liked her smile, when he could tease it out of her, a shy, self-conscious grin that revealed a genuine delight.

Moon took his wife in his arms. A cold wind rattled the windows and drove a heavy rain against the glass. Moon fiddled with the tiny pearl buttons of her dress.

How to begin.

"Jim?"

How to be young again, how to be kind. He was helpless against her eyes and the milky whiteness of her skin.

"Here." She took his hand, showing, leading, not because she knew anything about love, but because she didn't. Led him to the worn velvet daybed where, in rain, Moon relearned, or tried, the first sweet, shy secrets of love, and did begin, trailing the scent of it, fragrant from rain, she, did begin and beget Moon's only son, beneath the scowling family portraits: Mother Greentree, Father Greentree, Mae.

"And then he leaves her," the girl told the policeman.

"You're joking."

"Nope." She shook her head solemnly.

"A man like that's no better than a dog."

"He had his reasons."

Moon stared at the ceiling, the rough sod, the cottonwood beams. The bedroom was dark. Ross's collie, half a mile down the road, barked without commitment.

Moon rolled over and studied his wife's face. "This was back in the war."

She shifted beside him, sighed in her sleep. Moon reached out to stroke her hair and stopped himself for fear that his touch might wake her.

"Listen," he said.

Robert E. Lee had surrendered. Abraham Lincoln was dead. It was all over, Moon whispered, and yet, incredibly, as he and the others lounged in the sunlight of a warm April morning, a Mississippi Confederate boy and two zealous companions attacked the camp and, in the firing, wounded two Union soldiers.

Moon and the others were taken by surprise.

"Son of a bitch is crazy," someone said.

The rebels ran, and the Union troops pursued. Moon quickly outdistanced his comrades and came apace of the rebel boys, running for their lives yet in perfect joy. He heard their laughter and felt that he could almost trace, beneath their worn gray jackets, the intricate branching of their backs and their shoulder muscles. His arms, their arms, yearned forward together in the motion of effortless swimming. He was so close he could have reached out and tagged them, grabbing their collars, spinning them down, laughing the way boys do, but instead he stopped, and one of them, clearly the leader, slowed to a walk and glanced back over his shoulder.

The boy was blond, maybe seventeen, as finely made as a girl. His face had the calm innocence of an angel. Moon leaned over, his hands on his knees, fighting to catch his breath, and the boys stopped. The four of them were tucked in the curve of a lane where the woods grew thick. Sunlight filtered through the leaves and spattered their coats with gold. Moon and the blond boy studied each other, Moon, one-eyed now, wearing his homemade eye patch.

Moon held out his hand, whether asking the boy to surrender his weapon or offering some sort of recognition Moon didn't know.

"It's over," he said.

It seemed for a moment as though they might touch, but just then they heard the Union soldiers forty or fifty yards behind them, pounding down the road, and the rebels ran.

The Union forces cornered the boys in a graveyard. "Lee's a traitor," one of them cried. They waved a homemade flag, the stars and bars.

A row of Union troops knelt and loaded. "Give it up," Moon whispered across the grass.

The blond boy paced among the gravestones. Sunlight caught the granite and seemed to ignite it, as though the rebels were lost in a swirl of fire.

"Lay 'em down, boys," the captain called across.

The stones blazed in the sun. The lawn was a flat, even green, dotted by a brilliant white gazebo and beautiful in such a simple way that it broke Moon's heart. "Angel boy," Moon whispered. "Where you been?"

"Don't be foolish, now," the captain said.

They could have just laid down their weapons, walked forward, and lived free—the war was over—but Moon knew they would not. A dream had hold of those boys, all glow and glitter, the old raw deal. They were caught in some vanished, innocent landscape, and they would die for that country of their dreams.

A breeze lifted Moon's hair and ruffled his shirt. A silence had settled over the grass.

"Sir?"

"Take 'em alive if you can," the captain told the lieutenant.

"Take 'em alive, sergeant," the lieutenant said.

Moon's sergeant was a Davenport man called Rourke, an experienced soldier, easygoing and kind. He called out again to the boys, but they answered with fire.

"God damn it," the sergeant said.

He looked to the lieutenant, who looked to the captain.

The captain nodded.

The Union troops fired one synchronized round of two hundred shots. Moon discharged his weapon along with the rest. The blond boy stood forward of his companions and took the assault head-on.

The policeman was getting impatient. "You know more than you're letting on," he said.

"Think I killed him?"

"Possible."

"I wasn't even there."

He leaned toward the girl and spoke in a confidential voice. "Maybe it don't matter whether you did or whether you didn't. All that counts is what I say you did."

The girl pushed back from the table and stood up.

"Thinking it over now, are you?" he said.

His tenderness for her had cooled a bit. If the old geezer meant anything to her, she'd want to see him properly put in the ground. That was the way these girls were, though—heartless.

He flipped through the rest of Moon's diary. "Nothing but words." He stood up and eyed the girl. "Don't look to me like this old coot'd be worth the trouble it'd take to kill him off."

He tossed the diary into the fireplace.

The girl whirled around.

"What?" He looked up.

"Nothing."

He studied the girl. "I'm intending to burn this book." He took a box of matches from the mantelpiece, lit one, and watched her eyes. "How'd that be?"

She stood stiff and unyielding, barely breathing. "I'd like to keep it."

"But you can't read. Can you."

The girl said nothing.

He stuffed the book in his pocket. "Well, I'll just take it along, then."

"No!"

He peered at her closely. "Sure, there's something in there," he said. He handed it over. "Maybe you'd like to read it to me now."

She tried a smile. He wasn't buying. If he left, he'd probably take everything, and she'd never find out.

"Go on, girl."

She opened the book and pretended to find her place.

March 19, 1893
Dear Diary,
    It is a sweet Death, dying into her. Not a war Death, but a yielding up of Care, a long Rest and surely needed. Yet . . .

That something, anything, could dislodge him from this sweet and sleepy love seemed impossible, even to Jim Moon, but by April it was clear that things had changed.

Don't you love me, Jim?

Mae, content forever to be drowsing, floating down the scent of the other, warm, drifting in and out of sleep. Each day was like the last.

Don't you love me, Jim?

But how to begin.

"I'm hungry," the girl said. "Buy me some ham and eggs."

"Who do you think you're playing with, girl?"

"Buy me a plate of biscuits and gravy, then, and I'll show you one of the old boy's letters."

"You never spoke about any letters."

"Baking-powder biscuits and redeye gravy?"

Moon sat outside on a straightback chair, sketching, his good eye squinted in concentration. A marsh hawk was hunting along the fence, and Moon was determined to get him right. The wings were narrow, long, not as pointed as a falcon's, and held slightly lifted in a wide, shallow vee. It skimmed low—Moon sketched quickly—harrying some field mouse or shrew, then rose and circled and settled into a long, effortless glide. Moon had caught him just before the arc of that easy sweep, and now he reinforced the line, savoring, deepening it, as though he could take it in through his fingertips, that perfectly angled shape of wing.

Moon put down his pencil. "Mae?"

His long johns hung from a sagging clothesline. A few chickens scratched in the dirt by the woodpile. The sounds of domesticity—the chiming of tin dishes, a whispering broom—filtered out from the kitchen.

He missed her most when she was just steps away, when he could detect her presence only by sound.

"Mae?" he called. "Come out."

The broom stopped. "Are you drinking out there?"

Moon took a pull from a pint bottle and tucked it back in his pocket. "No."

"Are you sure?" she said.

The drinking was only partly despair. The drinking was also hope. But however it was, it grieved Mae Moon. Drinking was seeking the vision. When Moon drank—usually in the toolshed after supper—he saw a majestic landscape, America, glimpsed once in the midst of war and now almost forgotten. He saw the White City he read about in the papers.

"I won't come out if you're drinking. You know that."

Money didn't matter when Moon was drinking. Wives didn't sulk. Things went a little faster, smoother. Beauty had no cost. Ideas occurred to Moon when he drank, and he found obscure connections.

Mae appeared in the doorway, barefoot, wearing a white cotton apron that rode high over her belly. "What is it?" she said.

·　·　·

The girl held a blue willow plate in her left hand, heaped with biscuits and gravy, a yellowed page torn from a writing tablet in her right.

"'Dear Mae.'"

It was a rough draft. Moon had tinkered with the wording before he copied it over. Who knew where the final version was, most likely lost. The writing looked like little black worms, squirming, but Moon had read it to her so often she felt pretty sure that she could remember it.

"'You asked me if I love you and I surely do.'"

"Does that thing have an address?" The policeman grabbed for the letter.

"Hey." The girl snatched it back. "This here is my stuff. He left it to me."

"He left it *with* you. That's not the same thing."

The girl set the plate on the table and held the letter behind her back.

"Now, that's evidence there," he said. "You're obstructing justice."

She backed away. "Nowadays a girl has got to look out after herself."

Nights when Moon got to drinking, brooding, in tears sometimes, that wounded, and here she was—nothing to Moon, she imagined, but just a girl—playing games with his letter.

Jealous is all. How easy betrayal came. And what would she get in return? A little consideration from a cop.

The policeman paced the hotel room, passing back and forth through the dwindling wedge of sunlight that fell through the big east window. "Well, are you going to read that thing or not?"

The girl licked the gravy from her fingers.

"I can haul you in, you know," he said.

She hesitated a moment more.

"I'm not fooling with you."

"Oh, well, fiddle." Wasn't the whole wide world just one big betrayal? She held the letter up before her eyes and took a deep breath. "'You asked me if I love you—'"

"Slow down."

"'And. I. Surely. Do.'"

"You read that part already."

"I'm getting to the good." She cleared her throat. "'I love you so much.'" The girl rolled her eyes. "He *says*."

The policeman blew the girl a mocking kiss.

"'I love you more than anything.'" The girl stopped. "They always say that."

"Covers a world of possibilities."

"At first."

President Grover Cleveland took his place on the wooden platform. Moon could picture everything in his mind. Beside Cleveland stood Vice-President Stevenson and the noble Duke of Veragua, the lineal descendant of the heroic Italian mariner Christopher Columbus, whom they had come to honor. The president's cabinet was there in the White City, the diplomatic corps, members of the United States Congress, and the august board of directors of the exposition itself.

Two hundred thousand visitors had crowded into the fairgrounds. May the first, 1893. An early haze had burned off, the paper said, leaving the morning chilly and bright, the sky an opaque wash of pale blue.

Mr. Cleveland stepped forward and raised his hands. A cheer went up.

Ladies and gentlemen . . .

At the back of the crowd his voice must have seemed no more than a wavering echo, Moon imagined, but everyone would have been able to see the president smile and press a giant golden telegraph key, setting in motion a huge, complex machine.

The fountains burst forth. Veils fell from the statues. The fair's massive power plant came alive and began to throb, feeding energy through a network of cables. The crowd surged forward. In the crush, women fainted, babies began to cry. Cleveland took a shot of whiskey to keep away the cold, and Jane Addams, standing inattentively in the crowd, had her pocketbook stolen. Cheers and laughter. Fistfights broke out. *Ladies and gentlemen, Columbia!*

A glare of white. Children went wild with excitement. Adults felt giddy and rich and wise and uncertain. They laughed and cried and told one another that this was the dream come true, the end of care, the exaltation of power, Columbia.

Moon at that moment was sweeping out the barn. A dusting of straw had settled down on his shoulders and worked its way under his frayed collar. The sun was butter yellow over the outhouse, a dingy, cheerless glow on the empty horizon, and it was sinking. That night, Moon ate cold potatoes and greens by a kerosene lamp with Mae, teary and sullen, sitting across the table. And all the while, in Chicago, the Midway danced with light.

"Jackson Park wasn't no more than a swamp when they begun it." Moon pushed a dry crust of bread around his plate. "See here in the paper it says the land is all *reclaimed.*"

Mae said nothing.

"That means it's *new* land," Moon said. "Just made up out of marsh. Imagine that."

Mae stood up and began to clear the table.

"It's called engineering," Moon said.

There was work in Chicago, he told her. "All kinds. And I got experience."

There were easier, faster ways to get to be somebody than farming. Why, a man could make it overnight in a big city, come back home in one of Cobb's store-bought suits and live like a king. And then the stories he could tell. A clever young escape artist named Harry Houdini was working the Midway, a young piano player named Scott Joplin. Buffalo Bill was there and Gentleman Jim Corbett. Furthermore, Moon told Mae, a Mr. George Washington Gale Ferris from Pittsburgh had built a revolving wheel, taller than the Statue of Liberty, and forged an axle weighing forty-five tons. "The largest piece of steel ever forged by the hand of man," Moon said.

He fetched his copy of *Harper's Chicago and the World's Fair* from the sideboard. "Listen here," he said, and he read to her. "'This curiosity at Chicago is called "the Ferris Wheel." It is a wheel 250 feet in diameter, or as wide as twenty full-sized city dwellings. Its construction combines great strength with airy gracefulness and lightness by the adaptation of the principle upon which a bicycle wheel is built. The great circle, looking almost like a cobweb from a distance, will be revolved on an axle that will rest on two towers, each 150 feet high. On the periphery of the wheel, in the place where paddles would go on a paddle-wheel, will be hung twenty-six passenger-cars, each capable of seating sixty persons. These cars will be so adjusted as to keep their positions evenly and steadily while the great wheel revolves, and passengers will find themselves lifted far above the highest buildings, and commanding a view of the entire Exposition, the city, and a great segment of Lake Michigan's surface of emerald and sapphire.'"

"Who wants to ride on a wheel?" Mae said.

But Jim Moon could feel his body rising.

Summer came on. Mrs. Moon grew round. Moon made periodic trips up to Winterset to buy the Chicago papers. He clipped a series of guest articles, syndicated by the American Press Association, and read them to Mae over supper.

A hundred years hence, the experts predicted, the world would enter a golden age. Women would be equal to men. Moon winked at his wife. Air ships would navigate the skies. Taxation would be minimal, and longevity would be such that reaching one hundred and fifty years of age or more would be commonplace.

A senator from Kansas, a Populist, believed that men would grow wiser in the future. War would be abolished, and the nations would become one. A journalist asserted that the manifest destiny of America was to dominate, but that it would do so not by force or political intrigue but by the power of example. Life would become more complex, one writer argued. Another predicted that the trend of the next hundred years would be toward simplicity and honest living. Free trade, abundant energy, advances in science and education. Aluminum would replace iron, becoming the silver-white symbol of the new era. Opinions varied. All the writers agreed, though, that the nation had come of age. The fair in Chicago would herald the new, "American" century. By nineteen ninety-three, Moon read, the earth he knew would be a paradise.

Moon stopped reading and looked up.

"Why am I not enough for you?" Mae said.

Moon detected the scent of lavender, like a memory.

"I'm happy here," she said. "In *eighteen* ninety-three."

"I know, but listen." Moon opened his *Harper's.* "'A bazaar of many shops is another feature. Tents and dwellings are scattered about, and a host of the savage, swarthy, but picturesque people of Tunis and Algiers will fill the place with activity. Men, women, and children will compose the population, and will dance and play their music, cook and serve their food, and in every way illustrate their modes of life at home. Some native Arab fanatics will be among them, eating scorpions, carrying snakes familiarly about, cutting and piercing themselves with evil-looking weapons, and generally so behaving as to be interesting but totally unsuited to a family tea-party. The *dans de ventre*, which was so great a success in Paris, will be repeated here.'"

Moon closed the book and smiled. "It won't be a tea party," he said.

"Jim, I need to talk to you. With the baby coming—"

"It's *for* the baby."

"No."

"Listen." Moon thumbed through the guidebook, searching. "Just let me find my place."

July 6, 1893
Dear Diary,
    Corn's high. Likely start detasseling early if Weather holds. Mrs. Moon's health good. Columbus Ships have arrived all the way

from Spain & are anchored on Lake Michigan paper says. The white of their sails is brilliant as is entire City—all white. Dazzling paper says—a sight to behold.

P.S. These are not the real Ships of course.

Moon felt the days slipping away. He knew that the fair wouldn't wait. A glimpse of white—a whitewashed shed, a sheet of plain white writing paper—anything white seemed to tempt him. A son was born. Moon felt honored, frightened, caught, unworthy. The fair in Chicago had just three more months to run.

A month of tears and silent meals. Another of constant bickering. Weeks of colic and sleepless nights, and then one day, a hard, bright sun, a strong west wind, and for no better reason, Moon packed a change of clothes and his books in a dark green carpetbag, planning to leave quietly, without the complications of a goodbye.

Mae was still asleep. Moon tiptoed out of the bedroom and crossed the kitchen to the sideboard, where she kept a tablet of paper. He tore out a sheet and wrote:

Dear Mae,

You asked me if I love you & I surely do. I love you so much. I love you more than anything. There is no Other for me nor never could be one. I know I made Promises but there is a wondrous Fair in progress—a World's Fair—in Chicago & a magnificent City there all of white.

Mae there is such Hope. It is just for a week. I have taken a little Money from your cookie Jar to get me over the hump. Don't worry tho. If this Fair is all they say things will change.

Given this Deed I know I cannot make you see how very much I do love you. It seems to me sometimes I will break apart—split like dry wood or shatter like one of your Mama's china dinner plates in fondness for some simple thing you do. You hang a petticoat on the line or kneel down to fetch a piece of kindling & my heart twists up inside me & it is a funny thing Dear Heart but that old knot of Pain is sweet to me because I know it is my Love for you.

So don't ask me no more my Only Girl. I answer you Yes—now and for Always.

Your loving Husband,
James Ransom Moon

As it happened, Moon arrived in Chicago on the eve of Chicago Day, and all the hotels—the Great Northern, the Grand Pacific, the Windsor, the Saratoga, the Palmer, the Tremont—were full to capacity and then some. Those who couldn't get a cot in a hotel lobby walked all night or rented a chair for a dollar in some saloon, or, like Moon, they slept on the shore of Lake Michigan under the stars.

A family down from Milwaukee gave him some fried chicken and cornbread, a wedge of apple pie from the picnic basket, and Moon offered the father a drink of bourbon.

"Seen the fair?" the man said.

"Nope, not yet."

"This is our third visit."

Monday morning dawned bright and cloudless. There was a breeze off the lake. Moon got some coffee and started for Jackson Park. His back was stiff, and it felt good to walk. The Loop was crowded with out-of-towners: families with eager children; bewildered single men in off the farms, wary and gullible, their savings tucked inside their shoes. Working girls, brassy and dressed to the nines, walked down the sidewalk arm in arm.

The crowds for the Alley "L" were backed up at the Congress Street terminal, and the fair didn't even open till six-thirty. Every man in Chicago who owned a horse and wagon was freelancing transportation, but all the carts that passed Moon were mostly full.

At a street corner, a newsboy shoved a piece of paper into Moon's hand:

Proclamation!

WHEREAS, The 9th day of October, 1871, the City of Chicago was visited by a deluge of fire and almost wiped out of existence, which affliction carried its name around the world as the city of modern times which had suffered the most terrible calamity; and

WHEREAS, Since then Chicago has grown and prospered as no other city in the world had done in the same period of time, having added over six fold to its population and a hundred fold to its wealth; and

WHEREAS, Our citizens are desirous of showing the world their gratitude for the bountiful dispensation of Providence in allowing it to prosper so abundantly and have determined the 9th day of this month, the twenty-second anniversary of the great fire, to attend the World's Fair and make it the gala day of the Fair.

Therefore, To enable our people to evidence their gratitude to the Giver of all gifts, I, Carter H. Harrison, Mayor of Chicago, hereby request and advise all the business people of our city to abstain from work and lend their efforts towards making "Chicago day" the banner day of the World's Columbian Exposition.

Carter H. Harrison, *Mayor*

Moon decided to treat himself and take a lakeside steamer down to the fairgrounds. He walked to Van Buren and caught the whaleback excursion boat he had read about in the papers, the *Christopher Columbus*, built especially for the fair. She was a honey, sleek and roomy. Standing on the top deck, Moon could watch the city slip past, the streets opening one by one like the pages of a book. The old phoenix. He glimpsed elegant specialty shops and iron bridges, fancy department stores and handsome office buildings that rose to astonishing heights.

South of the Loop, the city fell away, melted into scrub grass, a sandy shoreline. Then, as the boat neared land again, a froth of white seemed to form out of nothing, a cloud, a cresting wave. The New Jerusalem. Buildings took shape. A white city, rising from the lake.

"Quite a sight."

Moon looked over. A little man in a derby hat was standing beside him, leaning on a bamboo cane. At first glance he seemed dapper, but Moon looked closely and noticed that the man's pants were greasy with age. His coat was threadbare.

"Just like Rome," the little man said. "Better, in fact." He flapped his arms. "Little more elbow room."

They landed at a broad pier. A movable sidewalk bumped them along to land. As they approached, a series of forty-eight white Corinthian columns rose from the water, flanking a massive triumphal arch—the Peristyle, the guidebook called it—beyond which the whole magnificent fair spread out before them. There was the long central pool Moon had read about in the papers, the Grand Basin, with French's towering *Statue of the Republic* at one end and MacMonnie's delicate work, *Columbian Fountain,* at the other. In between stood majestic buildings, white, intricately ornamented, one after another, each massive, each exactly the same height, a necklace of gleaming pearls around the basin, a froth of dreams, and all of it reflected in bright blue water.

"Echoes the Bosses' Farts."

"What?"

"Ecole des Beaux-Arts." The little man swept his white-gloved hand across the horizon.

"Oh," Moon said.

Moon's heart stopped. His lungs filled with water.

Darkness.

Quiet.

And then, emerging out of the gloom, buildings—glowing, wavering in the depths, a white city. It was what he had longed for, half expected, doubted, pursued, and it seemed to him now that he could enter and exit this city at will, moving like a fish in and out of the windows.

The buildings were so pure and unsullied they glowed, sugar castles, faintly defined by a delicate wash of shadows, and so exquisitely designed that, for all their massive domes, their graceful columns and ornamentation, they seemed to be weightless, floating on the lagoon.

"It's like a paradise," Moon said, turning toward his companion. But Moon was alone. The strange little man who had dogged his steps from the pier had suddenly vanished.

"A man who's truly in love would never leave," the policeman said.

"Depends on what it is he's in love with."

"You've got an answer for everything," he said.

"I wish."

"Read me the last of it."

"'October 9, 1893.'" The girl barely looked at the page. "'Dear Diary. It is like a Dream come true & I am at the Center. Me. Myself. Jim Moon.'"

After an hour or so at the fair, Moon abandoned his guidebook. It was beyond words, a city of light. The whiteness was accented with splashes of color—banners, flowers, flags of all nations—and everywhere he turned there were happy couples and pretty girls. The fair had attracted the best and the worst America had to offer, a varied assortment of confidence men and dandies, spiritualists and genius inventors, educators, scholars, gamblers, penny-ante entrepreneurs and lunatic preachers, fops, famous sportsmen, newspaper stringers and snake-oil salesmen, actors, foreign dignitaries, businessmen, and old-maid schoolteachers looking for wealthy husbands. There were restaurants and beer gardens, soda-water stands and souvenir shops—Moon stopped at every one. He bought a cranberry glass pitcher for Mae at the Libbey Glassware Pavilion and had her name etched on the side along with the words "World's Columbian Exposition, Chicago" and the date. He missed her, at first, longed for his wife so deeply that he could almost feel her hand in his and hear her footsteps, echoing his on the pavement.

He bought a Chicago Day badge; a paper fan, lithographed with a bird's-eye view of the fair; a photograph of Daniel Burnham, Director of Works, the organizing genius behind the fair. He also acquired a steel engraving of Ellen Terry as Lady Macbeth; a souvenir Christopher Columbus fifty-cent piece; a little key-wound tin Ferris wheel for Win; an Irish lace handkerchief; the *Inter Ocean* Chicago Day special edition.

"Come with me, Mr. Moon. Come to the Midway Plaisance. Plaisance, plaisance. Pleasure."

The little man was watching Moon from a rooftop promenade.

"We'll go after dark," he whispered. "We'll go on a dare. Laughing to keep our courage up. There's nothing to fear in the dark anymore. Is there?"

The little man popped up at Moon's elbow. "I see you're enjoying yourself."

"Says here," Moon said, perusing a schedule of the day's events, "that Mayor Carter Harrison will 'extol the distinctions of Chicago, past and present,' and ring the New Liberty Bell at high noon."

"Wonderful."

"At two o'clock, 'schoolchildren in colorful costumes and carrying the flags of the various states will assemble at the Peristyle and march around the basin in a special Reunion of States parade,'" Moon continued, "which is 'intended to heal the divisions of the war.'"

"Patriotic songs will be sung," the little man added.

At three o'clock, the elderly Simon Pokagon, chief of the Pottawatomie, would deliver a speech, "The Red Man's Columbian Greeting," and hand over the deed to Chicago, purchased from the tribe, Moon read, in 1833 for three cents an acre.

"Too bad we never got around to paying them boys."

Moon by then was used to the high-flown rhetoric of the fair and could rattle off fancy descriptions on his own that rivaled the ornate prose in his guidebook. "The stately, high-domed Administration Building, centerpiece of the fair," he announced, "towers majestically at the far western end of the Grand Basin."

"You got it," the little man said. "Chicago style."

"It is abundantly adorned," Moon went on, "for the instruction of the masses with artfully sculpted allegorical figures—Earth, Air, Fire, and Water—each depicted in its wild and in its civilized state."

They circled the building. Fire Controlled, they noted, displayed a fearful demon tumbled at the foot of a powerful blacksmith, and poised above, a goddess lifting her torch.

"Ever see fire?" the little man said. "Close up?"

"Some."

The little man tugged at his celluloid collar, displaying mottled, melted flesh. "Chicago, 1871. Was you there?"

Moon shook his head.

"You will be," he said.

A dry summer, a dry fall, Sunday evening, the whole sprawl of Chicago a tinderbox. Plank roads and wooden bridges, stables and wooden tenement buildings with tar and pine-chip roofs. A city on the edge of sleep, waiting for a spark.

The little man was conducting business on the QT in Conley's Patch, a row of cheap saloons and brothels on the South Side, when he heard the alarm.

"De Koven Street," somebody said. "A cowshed's burning."

"Is *that* all."

Flames caught the straw and grabbed hold, fingered their way through the clapboard walls.

"No, this one's a beauty, a big burn."

"I gotta see." The little man grabbed his money and clapped his derby hat on his head.

By that time the fire was on the move, running along the fences, grabbing hold. Sparks, lifted, pushed along by the wind, caught the wood-shingled roofs of neighboring houses, igniting block after block.

The little man was delighted. He chased it along. The fire jumped the river, and he ran after it. It took the gasworks, the Palmer House, running up Wabash Avenue, State. The post office, the *Tribune* building. Burning debris fell like a red snow.

The little man's celluloid collar caught fire, ignited by a shower of sparks. He pulled it off with his bare hands, tossed it aside, and kept on running.

The wind seemed to be blowing from every quarter. At the courthouse the prisoners howled in the darkness. They said it couldn't burn, but there it was. Limestone melted like butter frosting. The bell in the tower was sounding its own knell.

Livery stables went up, and horses, mad with fear, galloped wild in the streets. There was looting, fighting. Whiskey from broken barrels ran in the gutters. They said it would never reach the North Side, but it rushed on, crossing the river again—the reaper factory, Lill's Brewery, Unity Church—leaving a strange lull in the streets where it had passed.

Now the houses of the rich—Kinzie, Ogden, Newberry, Rumsey. Funny what they saved: a family portrait, a cooking stove, a basket of newborn kittens, scraps of silk for a crazy quilt, a marble clock, a new straw hat. In one street a woman knelt, holding a silver cross above her head, praying to God, the hem of her skirt on fire. Sparks rained down, igniting the plank roads, turning them into rivers of flame. Bridges collapsed. Men and women and children, driven on by the heat, pushed by the crowds, reached the shoreline and waded into the lake.

"So, that was the fire," Moon said.

"Yep. She was a dandy."

A cold October drizzle began early on the morning after the fire. The little man stood up and stretched and brushed the sand from his trousers. Someone had soaked a rag in lake water and wrapped it around his throat while he slept—some good Samaritan. He put on his hat and raked it low over one eye. Along the horizon a thin rim of pale gold light simmered on the lake.

A woman found her smoking feather bed and salvaged enough down to make two new pillows. The grain elevators were still intact, the lumber district, the stockyards, most of the factories, the railroad lines, and that was hope. Somehow a father procured a pitcher of milk for his children's breakfast. Somebody made coffee from parched rye.

The young woman on the Midway had a Kodak.

"How'd you sneak that in?" the little man said.

"I know somebody." She smiled. "Who knows somebody."

She was tall and slender, blond, remarkably pretty. She wore a black skirt and a white eyelet blouse with mutton-leg sleeves, a black straw hat with a purple ribbon. But it was more her attitude that struck Moon.

"The big boys don't like nobody taking pictures," the little man told her. "Like to keep control of them images."

"I don't always do what the big boys say."

Moon smiled. Brassy. He liked her.

"Take my picture," the little man said. "Over by Hagenbeck's animal show, me and my good friend Ioway."

"Silly," she said. Her eyes were flirtatious. "It's almost dark."

"That don't matter. Anything's possible here."

The girl demurred.

"Tomorrow then. Meet us."

"I don't know."

"Oh, come on."

"My brother doesn't like me to talk to strangers."

The little man grinned. "I'm not a stranger," he said.

At twilight a torchlight parade, featuring Miss Elizabeth A. Flynn as the "I Will" maiden, had circled the Grand Basin, to be followed shortly by fireworks, ignited from several points—the lakefront, the lagoon, the Court of Honor, the Wooded Island.

"The fair's even more beautiful at night," the young woman said. "Don't you think so, Mister . . . ?"

"Moon."

"Mr. Moon."

"I do."

"He was in love with somebody," the girl in the hotel said.

"Who? You, then?"

"Not hardly. Some girl from that city, I guess. I don't know her name."

The policeman wrote everything down.

Light. Illuminating the Court of Honor, revealing, distorting, dancing on water. Light tracing the symmetry of the buildings, casting a glow. Giant searchlights, boats bedecked with lights, glittering, skimming across the lagoon.

And fireworks! The lake came alive with color—crimson, silver, sapphire.

"What's your name?" the little man asked the young woman.

"I'm not in the habit of giving my name to strangers."

"I'll just call you Claire, then," the little man said.

A brightness opened above them. Rockets exploded and died away, leaving ghostly chrysanthemums that faded as they fell. The woman looked up, revealing the perfect white slope of her throat.

The policeman wrote, "Possible motive: unrequited love."

"Win," Caroline said, "where's Serbia?"

There was a war in Europe. Caroline could talk of little else. She folded the Winterset newspaper and laid it beside her breakfast plate. "President Wilson is neutral," she explained, "but some people say it's just a matter of time till we'll be in it."

"My late husband fought at San Juan Hill," Mrs. Maythorpe said, seating herself at the head of the table.

"Mama, he did not," Caroline said. "He was a cook."

"He was a soldier," Mrs. Maythorpe said. "He was right in the thick of it."

"Well, he didn't fight," Caroline said. "Daddy was shot in the head while he was making mulligan stew," she told Winslow. She plopped a dollop of marmalade on her toast. "Of course, he's still a hero. All soldiers are."

The thought of war made Winslow's stomach flip.

"They say the big guns do terrible damage," Caroline said. Her eyes glistened. "They say the men are blown to smithereens."

"Excuse me." Win folded his napkin and left the table.

The air off the lake was clean and crisp—a gorgeous morning. Sunlight flooded the fairgrounds. Moon had acquired a skimmer hat, which he wore at a rakish angle, and as he walked he practiced saluting the ladies.

"Just look at those buildings," Moon remarked to a startled passerby.

"I see 'em."

"Shining like alabaster."

Moon was on his way to meet Claire on the Midway. She had made quite an impression the night before. He felt lighthearted and figured he might just treat her to ice cream.

"Hey, looky here." A young man grabbed Moon's arm. "I just found me a bundle."

Sure enough, the young man, clearly a country boy, had a gentleman's leather wallet in his hand.

"Any name?" Moon asked him.

The wallet was fat with greenbacks. The young man was excited. "I just happened to look down, and there she was on the walkway."

"Must be a hundred dollars in that poke," Moon said.

"What do you think I should do?"

Another man heard them talking and wandered over. "Find something?"

"This fellow here found a passel of money," Moon informed him. "Ain't that something?"

The second man was well-dressed and polished. "Perhaps I can be of assistance. My name is Augustus Barkley. I'm an attorney." He handed the country boy his card.

"What do you think I should do?"

"Why, turn it in, of course. Over at the Administration Building."

"Think so?"

"Absolutely." This Barkley seemed pretty sure of himself. "I would imagine there's a substantial reward. Wouldn't you say so, sir?" He turned to Moon.

"Gosh," the fellow said.

"Looks like this is your lucky day," Moon said.

"Yeah, but . . ." The fellow glanced around him, nervous. He twisted his cap in his hands.

"Is there a problem?" Barkley said.

"Well, the thing is, I'm supposed to meet my girl," the fellow said. "And I'm late now."

"Say, that *is* a problem," Barkley said.

He and the country fellow scratched their heads and studied the ground. What to do, what to do. They paced up and down a little. A fellow couldn't just chase off to return a missing wallet and still be able to meet his girl on time.

"And she's awful particular if I'm late," the fellow said.

"You should return it in a timely fashion," Barkley said, "but of course . . ."

"*I* could do it," Moon said.

The other two men looked at each other and smiled.

"There you go," Barkley said. He and the country fellow shook Moon's hand. "Settled."

"Wait a minute," the fellow said. His face pinched into a mask of suspicion. "What about my reward?"

"Oh, yes, of course, certainly. I'd almost forgotten." Barkley considered for a moment, cupping his chin in his hand. "Why, you could split it," he said. "Half for you and half for—what did you say your name was?"

"Moon."

The country fellow deliberated. "How do I know I can trust him?"

Barkley seemed mildly astonished. "Why, I'm sure Mr. Moon is an honest man. He looks honest enough. You *are* an honest man?" he said to Moon.

Moon nodded.

"There. See? Solid as a dollar."

Moon began to reconsider. "I don't know," he said. "I don't want to be carrying a big wad of money around."

"Certainly not. The place is thick with thieves. No, here's what you do," Barkley said. "Give me your money, sir."

Moon hesitated.

"You'd better give it to me if you don't want to lose it."

Moon obliged. He had about forty dollars.

Barkley tucked Moon's money inside the wallet and hid it inside the country fellow's shirt. "Hide it inside like this." He patted the boy's chest and drew out the wallet again. "They'll never even know it's there."

He handed Moon the wallet. "Now all you two need to do is arrange where to meet to split the reward—I'd suggest the entranceway to the Agriculture Building. Say, one o'clock?" He patted Moon on the back. "You go a little bit out of your way, and you're both richer men for the adventure."

Moon smiled and nodded. "I'll be there."

The policeman crossed the room and opened the window. Street noise floated up to them. "Air's like a damn blast furnace," he said.

The girl was watching him. He felt her eyes on the back of his neck.

"So, what else?" he said, turning.

"Just the drawings."

"Nothing else?"

"Well, he had these lists." The girl took a crumpled piece of paper from the nightstand. "Lots of lists, and he used to read them out to me." She cleared her throat and began to recite: "Frederick Jackson Turner, historian. Elias Disney, carpenter. T. Roosevelt. Eugene V. Debs, Samuel Gompers, labor leaders. Dwight Moody, preacher."

"I know those names. Some."

"Clarence Darrow. John Dewey. William Jennings Bryan. Susan B. Anthony. Booker T. Washington. Ida B. Wells. Frederick Douglass."

"Let me see that."

"Painters," the girl went on. "Winslow Homer. John Singer Sargent. William Merritt Chase . . ." Her voice wavered and gave out in the heat.

The policeman snatched the list from the girl's hand. "So," he said, "all these famous people, they lived in this white city."

The girl scowled. "Didn't I just tell you that?"

"Remember the name?"

"Nope."

"Can't do much about shipping him home if we don't know where to ship him."

The thin wedge of sunlight had vanished. The room was so hot the policeman unbuttoned his collar. "You'd do right to think about helping me, girl." He looked at her hard. "There'll be expenses."

"Like what?"

"Funeral, burial plot, that fancy tombstone with the book and all. You know, you might just end up getting stuck with this old man."

"How?" she said.

"By default."

Claire was waiting on the Midway. Moon's heart ached in his chest when he saw her.

"Ain't she pretty?" The little man had appeared out of nowhere. "All dressed up like Mrs. Astor's pet pony."

71

"Where'd you come from?" Moon said.

"Oh, I been out walking around, up and down, to and fro, getting the lay of the land."

"Hello, Ioway," Claire said.

The little man stepped between them. "Don't go getting any ideas now, Moon." He took Claire's arm. "You neither, missy," he said. "Not till you seen everything."

"Oh?"

"Not till you seen *me*."

Moon pulled the little man aside. The wallet, of course, had been switched, and the duplicate that Moon had been left holding contained a stack of newspaper, cut to the size of currency and wrapped in two or three genuine dollar bills.

"The old handkerchief trick," the little man said.

"What am I going to do?"

"You'll recover."

"But that was my wife's money."

Moon told him a little about his life, the Greentree place, his time in the war. "I can't fail again."

"Moonie, look around you. Take it all in slow, and what do you see?"

Moon was bewildered.

"This is the land of opportunity, Moon."

Caroline's romance with the war did not distract her from the business of the stone. She continued to work away, bashing it, sometimes just in passing, with whatever implement was handy. Every morning she hit it a few licks before she started the day's chores. She gave it a few more after supper.

"You just refuse to take any responsibility for this thing, don't you?" she said to Win one morning, pausing after a few swings of the sledgehammer. Jim Moon's stone had come between them.

"Maybe we could bury it," Winslow suggested.

"Bury it?"

"Maybe we don't have to bust it up. Maybe we could just hide it somewhere, put it out of sight and not have to think about it anymore."

"Winslow," Caroline said, "we cannot bury a stone four feet long. We'd be digging for days. Besides, it would still *be* there."

She sat down on the porch step and mopped her brow. "I wish it would sink right down," she said. "I wish it would sink right down to hell." This, of course, was the least of her expectations.

"Well . . ."

"Dynamite." She jumped up. "That's what we need. We've been going at this thing all wrong."

"Where would you get dynamite?" Winslow said.

"Oh, I'll get it all right."

Winslow imagined the stone lifting into the air, shattering, and raining down as rubble. "Don't you think that's kind of extreme?" he said.

"This thing has caused enough confusement."

A Street in Cairo was the hit of the fair. For a quarter, visitors to the Midway could wander past painted mosques and ornate houses, even a scale replica of the ancient temple of Luxor. There were camel rides and street magicians, dark, sullen people in strange garb.

"They say them dancing girls is something to see," the little man said. "Dance with their bellies—oops, pardon. With their *midriffs* exposed."

Moon studied the girls loitering outside the entrance to the theater and listened to the babble of ballyhoo. Plump and sleepy-eyed, with ropes of amber beads around their necks, the girls wore gauzy trousers and red leather slippers, jeweled caps and bright velvet jackets with gold coins sewn to the hems.

"Wanna take a peek?" the little man said.

"Why not?" Claire said. "Let's be bold, for once."

Moon was reluctant.

"C'mon. Take your mind off your troubles," the little man said.

"Fahima, Sadiga, Hahnim, Zakia." The names of the girls rolled off the pitchman's tongue.

"Just two bits," the little man said. "A bargain at twice the price."

"Ain't you forgetting something?" Moon said. He turned his pockets inside out. Nothing but a dirty handkerchief, a carpenter's pencil, a length of string, lint, the leather-bound diary, and his Christopher Columbus souvenir half-dollar.

"Listen, Moon, tomorrow's another day. I told you—get it, spend it, lose it, make it all back and then some. This here's America, rube."

"My wife was right," Moon said. "I ain't got the sense of a newborn calf."

"You are green."

"Boys, come on." Claire was getting impatient.

The little man dragged Moon in by the arm. "Hey, a little looksee won't never hurt you, Moon." He stuffed three or four dollars in Moon's pocket.

The theater was larger than Moon had expected, and crowded with men. The stage was draped with rich, mustard-yellow satin, and wooden chairs were provided. Moon, Claire, and the little man took seats in the second row. There was a scent in the air—like cinnamon, Moon thought, or clove. Five musicians, holding various drums and flutes, sat cross-legged on a low wooden platform. One made a tambourine hiss. One played a stringed instrument, something like a mandolin, plucking it with his fingers and singing in a high-pitched wail. The girls came out from behind a tapestry side curtain and undulated across the stage. They wore brass bells on their ankles and kept a nervous, intricate rhythm with finger cymbals raised above their heads. A swirl of color, the girls twisting, smiling, their eyes glittering, black, the heat of the close theater. Moon felt weak.

One exotic beauty caught Moon's eye, flashed him a smile, twirling, and flirted coyly over her shoulder. Her teeth were stained and her eyes outlined in kohl, and when she raised her hands above her head, the curve of her breasts and her soft dark waist exposed, Moon saw a silver dazzle. His head went light. A brief darkness swept over him, and sweat popped out on his brow.

"Drop them veils," the little man shouted. He stood up and clamped his cigar in his teeth, hoochie-cooched toward the stage, and the dark girl flashed him the same seductive smile she had given Moon.

Claire was the only woman in the audience. She laughed and stretched out her arms and shook her shoulders, imitating the dancers.

"Atta girl," the little man said.

Moon dug his fingernails into the palms of his hands. He was astonished. Claire's laughter was raucous, forward. Moon had never seen a girl so brassy. Mae would have blushed and hidden her face. Mae would have never even—Mae. Moon pictured his wife, the baby resting on her hip, holding the empty cookie jar. *Jim?* The music stopped.

Flimflammed.

Hornswoggled.

The oldest trick in the book.

The girls disappeared in a shimmer of red and amber.

"Whoo-ee!" the little man said. "That's dancing."

The three of them emerged from the theater, blinking in the sunlight. "Some show, rubes," the little man said.

They strolled west, past the captive balloon, the ostrich farm. At the military encampment they turned back, the little man and Claire in the lead and Moon, gloomy, trailing a step behind.

"What's the matter with your friend?" Claire said.

"Old Moon? Just got an education is all. Learned to recognize a Michigan roll."

The Midway was an eyeful, hawkers on every side. Beer gardens and flower girls and replicas of all the world's great wonders. Donegal Castle, Sitting Bull's Cabin. Natives from Borneo, Fiji, Java, the Sandwich Islands. Filipinos, Germans, Chinese, Arabs,

Nubians, Sudanese. The Tomb of Thi, the Blarney Stone. The Ferris Wheel.

"Oh, let's," the girl said. "Jim?"

Beneath the muddy currents of the river Moon opened his one good eye. Life on the surface—the painted boats, the arrogant boys who jumped from the docks, laughing, the rocking waves—created a rhythm that throbbed downward. Life again, ragged and full of longing. Moon danced.

"Love, love, love," the policeman said.

"Don't make fun, now. He was a sweet old boy."

"But who was he at all?" he said. "And did he have gainful employment?"

The girl drifted back to the window. Just explain the man, that was what he was saying. Tell him, quick and simple, how Moon ached to live in beauty, how he thought he had it there for a while. The girl didn't have any words for that. And anyway this cop wouldn't understand.

"Give me something, girl, or I'll haul you in."

"All right, then. He was a messenger."

This got the cop's attention. "Delivering what? For who?"

The girl shrugged.

"Letters? Packages?"

"He didn't say."

"So where do you live, Claire?" the little man said. "Live with your mama?"

"No."

They were strolling along the Court of Honor.

"Live alone? With a lady friend? One of them boarding houses?"

"I live with my brother and his wife."

"Where at?"

"In Pullman Town."

Pullman was south of Chicago, a planned workers' city on Lake Calumet. It was built by George Pullman, a self-taught inventor, the man who raised the Matteson Hotel six feet out of the mud, the practical philanthropist, the railroad car man.

"Well, we'll have to come and see you sometime," the little man said.

They wandered all afternoon, the little man with Claire by the arm and Moon, silent and moody, trailing behind them. They were totally different, Moon and the little man, but despite a few reservations, Claire liked them both. Moon brought out a tenderness in her—a sentimental man, easily wounded, fragile, almost like a boy. And as for the little man, he had such energy and was so full of talk, every moment with him seemed like an adventure. They took a gondola ride and toured the grounds on the elevated railroad. At Claire's insistence, they visited the Woman's Building, where they saw the work of Mary Cassatt. The little man's comments made Claire laugh, a sound that nudged old Moon in new directions.

Inside the vast Manufactures and Liberal Arts Building they inspected precision watches and fine musical instruments, tapestries, Belgian lace and English china, enamelwork and gold jewelry, gemstones, fabrics of every description from Oriental silk to common American homespun. There was soap and soda, pharmaceuticals, clothing, coffins. "It's too much," Claire said.

The work of artisans from around the world was on display, ornaments wrought in amber, bronze, meerschaum, pearl, jade, ivory. Bohemian glassware, cloisonné vases, lacquerware and inlaid boxes, silver, porcelain, earthenware.

The little man bought Claire a star-shaped garnet pin.

"I really couldn't accept it," she said.

The little man insisted. "A trifle." He pinned it on her collar.

The Casino Pier, the Peristyle. In a replica of the Franciscan monastery of La Rabida, where, four hundred years before, an eager, uncertain Christopher Columbus, deep in his plans, had awaited an audience with Queen Isabella, they saw the first known map of the New World.

In every building there were wonders. Agriculture, forestry, mining, fine arts. In the Electricity Building they saw the tower of light, the telephone, a teleautograph for transmitting facsimile drawings by telegraph, the elevator, the phonograph, even an electric chair designed for humane executions.

"Good old Yankee ingenuity," the little man said.

Electricity would change the world—everybody said so—but it was Machinery Hall, a tribute to mass force, that seemed to Moon most American. Boilers, pumps, engines. The smell of burning oil. Machines for working metal and cutting stone. Looms and printing presses and stamping machines. The throb of power. Machines for electroplating, forging, welding. Machines to cut and grind, weigh and measure, manufacture—paper, nails, rope—even machines to make machines. It was terrifying, fascinating. Moon had his doubts, but the little man was enchanted.

They wandered from building to building and saw it all. How cigarettes are made in Egypt, how a water mill works. Modern methods of fighting fires. The history of man from prehistoric times down to the present. There was the largest nugget of gold in existence, the world's largest canary diamond, a bust of Germany's William the Second, the famous Venus de Milo sculpted in chocolate. A two-headed pig, fifty thousand red roses in bloom, the Yerkes telescope. It was all there. The biggest, the most, the oldest, the latest. The greatest gun of this or any age.

"Here's the story of your hometown," the little man said to Claire. Moon leaned in to take a look.

They were passing the Transportation Building, where the Pullman Pioneer and other railroad cars were on display. The little man picked up a pamphlet and read it. "Says here Pullman is a town where everything 'ugly and discordant' has been eliminated." He winked. "And everything that promotes family stability, health, thrift and 'cleanliness of thought' has been provided."

He threw the pamphlet back on the stack. "Cleanliness of thought ain't quite in my line."

There was a plaster of Paris model of the town. "Here's where we live," Claire said. "And there's the embroidery department where I work, and Billy's department, and this is the Arcade."

"Won't be working there long."

"What do you mean?"

"Hell's fire, girl, where you been? Depression. Hard times. All over the country. This here fair?" The little man swept his bamboo cane in a broad half circle. "Illusion!"

"No," Moon said.

"Hell, a good strong wind would blow this place away. The 'planned' city, the 'white' city. Go on into the Loop, rubes. They's beggars walking the streets, hungry kids and desperate women. Open your eyes, girlie. That's the city."

"My brother makes almost six hundred dollars a year," Claire said. "The plant is strained to capacity."

"Who told you that?"

Moon looked around him. Illusion.

"Strained to capacity." The little man spit on the sidewalk. "By winter, old man Pullman'll be selling below cost."

Claire was offended. "I don't believe you," she said.

"Well, missy, not everyone does," he said. "Not right at first."

The policeman folded Moon's lists and tucked them in his pocket. "Anything else?"

She hesitated.

"Come on, now."

The girl brought out a stack of dark, smudgy charcoals: monstrous machinery, masses of wheels and gears and levers, illogically connected. The machines belched fire and smoke, and human figures cowered before them, serving.

"Like I told you, he was a little bit touched."

"Lost in his wits, was he?"

The girl nodded. "He'd get to drinking and talk about the buildings."

"What did he say?"

"Showed me a bunch of stuff, a four-bit piece and this photograph he had—must of been took in Africa. And he's leaning—"

"What did he say about the *buildings?*"

"He said they were hollow."

The White City, seemingly ancient and solid, was, Moon soon discovered, a clever illusion, constructed of a material called staff, which was plaster and straw or hemp mixed together and applied to wooden slats or laths laid over an iron framework. The buildings mimicked stone but were in fact nothing more than elaborate sheds. Viewed from the inside, they revealed their iron skeletons and seemed to Jim Moon like enormous cages.

"Cages!" The little man scowled. "Why, hell's fire, boy, this here's a miracle. Largest building ever constructed by man. Three million board feet of lumber, five railroad carloads full of nails."

The Manufactures and Liberal Arts Building of Mr. Post was an engineering marvel—the guidebook confirmed it. Of such dimensions that one might fit the Great Pyramids of Egypt, the United States Capitol building, Winchester Cathedral, and Saint Paul's as well inside it handily and still have room left over for Madison Square Garden.

"But that's just . . . big." Moon was confused.

"Well," the little man said, "there's visions and visions."

A full moon hung low over Sweetbriar. Mother Maythorpe sat in the parlor embroidering a fancy pillow sham, but Caroline, exhausted by swinging the sledgehammer, had gone up to bed early.

It wasn't that she didn't love Win—in her own way. Hadn't she been practically faithful for two whole years? But Win was not the only fish in the ocean, and a girl nowadays had to think about her future.

Caroline turned down the patchwork quilt and crawled into bed. Truth to tell, Win was not the best-looking boy she had ever gone with, and he was certainly far from the brightest. He wasn't rich or cultured; he had no family. Nothing, in other words, to recommend him. She plumped up her pillow, pounding it with her fists. Surely to goodness, she could do better.

She blew out the candle beside her bed, and moonlight flooded the room. On the other hand, he was kind of cute. That curly hair and those big blue eyes. She smiled. Win was raw material, so to speak, so dull and serious, she thought, that he certainly would do something grand with his life, once he found himself.

Meanwhile Winslow sat on the back porch steps, turning a fragment of limestone in his hands. The Book of Life lay open in the moonlight.

Dynamite.

Something stirred in the grass—a beetle, a grasshopper, prey for the bats and the nighthawks. A nervous wind teased a cloud across the moon.

Where would you . . .

Oh, I'll get it all right.

Win stood up and studied the stone. A monstrosity. Well, maybe it was. It sure had the new worn off of it now, thanks to Caroline. Win wondered if he even cared. Noble Jim Moon. What kind of hero leaves his family for some old amusement park?

Moon's drawings troubled the policeman—their nightmare vision. "Was it the drink or what was it at all, making him see such as this?" he asked the girl.

"I think the hard drinking come later."

"A tragic man, then."

"Yes and no," she said.

How to explain Moon. The girl considered. How to explain herself, for that matter. How she was shipped to a couple in New Jersey and how, for reasons she never knew, they changed their minds. Sent her on to an orphanage upstate. St. Joseph's Asylum. When she got out—just turned sixteen—she wandered down to Manhattan with Tommy Keil. Moon stopped them on Broadway one day and admired her garnet pin.

"Where'd you get that?" Moon said.

"Who wants to know," said Tommy.

Tommy started to pull her away, but Moon put up his dukes. "Leave her be," he said. "I know that star."

And what did *she* know? Nothing. Except that the pin was in a box of linens and other essentials the sisters gave her the day they turned her loose. "Came in when you came in," somebody told her. "Your mother's estate."

They were strolling along the Court of Honor, the little man and Claire up ahead and Moon trailing behind them, as usual, brooding, when a Columbian Guard stopped them.

The little man was carrying Claire's camera.

"Got a permit for that thing?"

"Thing?"

"Gotta have a permit," the guard said, "signed and sealed by C. D. Arnold himself. No permit, no camera."

The little man was brash, arrogant, always putting himself in charge, and Moon didn't like that much. Sure, the fellow was generous, had given Moon a buck or two, but—and this was mighty suspicious—he refused to tell them his right name. First he told Claire he was T. J. Nickels, but it was a different story every time. Once it was Nicholas J. Nickels, and he told Moon to call him Tom, Dick, and Harry, Morris the Mole, Chicago Charlie, Nick, Red, and Moon didn't know what all. Every now and then this Nick would sit down and write a few notes in a big red leather-bound book he carried— Moroccan leather, he told them it was—and wouldn't show Moon or Claire what it was he was writing.

"Why don't you run along," the little man told the guard.

"I'm doing my job."

"Maggot! You little turd! Mess with me? I'll rip your guts out, boy." The little man handed the camera to Moon.

"Mr. Nickels, please," Claire said.

"Permit, my patootie! You don't know who you fooling with. Here!"

The little man gave the guard a shove, and he fell backward and sprawled on the walkway.

"That's the force of righteous indignation," the little man said.

The guard looked up, bewildered. "Who are you, anyhow?"

Win Moon was not a well-built man. His arms and legs were scrawny, like his father's, and he had what the doctor who brought him into the world had called a "hole" in his chest, a deep depression almost the size of a fist beneath his breastbone. Nevertheless, he managed to roll the gravestone out of Mrs. Maythorpe's yard, down the gravel road, and up the little rise beyond the church. He was delighted to find that once he got it rolling—he used a two-by-four to nudge it along—the stone tumbled easily.

He rolled it past the graveyard and out into a cornfield, where the stalks concealed it. The field belonged to Eule Seymour, and Winslow reasoned that by the time Seymour found the stone—maybe around harvest in late September—circumstances might have changed somehow.

"Stolen!" Mother Maythorpe yelped. She had stepped out onto the porch the following morning to shake out the tablecloth and discovered that overnight Moon's tombstone had disappeared. "Win, you should notify the sheriff."

"He don't want it, Mama," Caroline said. She was still at the kitchen table, reading the war news in the Winterset paper. "Good riddance to bad rubbage, I say."

Win stood up and stretched. "I don't guess I'll bother," he said casually.

Caroline stopped reading and looked up. She pulled her lower lip into a pout and blew her hair away from her eyes. "Well, I don't guess so," she said.

Evening was settling over the fairgrounds. Pretty soon the lights would be coming on. The Ferris wheel had stopped turning for lack of passengers, and the kiosk vendors had taken advantage of the lull in the day to sit in the spill of dying light that flooded the Court of Honor. Roller-chair attendants dozed in their chairs, and visitors, exhausted, elated, pestered by cranky children, wondered whether to stay for the fireworks. The sun, a huge, theatrical sun, burning orange, was sinking on the horizon when Moon and Claire and the little man found themselves back in Cairo.

"Take our picture, Claire," the little man said. "Me and old Cornpone here. Get in real close."

The little man stood next to Moon, the two of them in front of the arching gate. The sun was behind them. A camel wandered by. Claire pointed and smiled. She waved her hand. "Move in closer," she said.

"This'll be something to show your grandkids—you and me at the fair." The little man nudged Moon in the ribs. "Hook your arm up over my shoulder," he said. "Lean into me. Two pals, old buddies, off on a tear in the Windy City—that's the ticket. Now give her a great big smile."

Moon reluctantly hoisted his elbow up over the little man's shoulder.

"That's a keeper."

Moon looked left at the little man and smiled.

"Tell me his name," the policeman said, "or you're going in to the station."

"He was the man in the moon."

"Now don't be cute."

Once he found her, Moon wouldn't let her go. Moving from hotel to hotel, from bar to bar. The Village, all around the Lower East Side, then Jersey and back, up to the Bronx, Brooklyn Heights—Moon liked to look at the bridge. And all the time reading the diary, the guidebook, the poetry, getting more and more lost in memories. He held her hand whenever they went out—*Afraid to lose you again.* He brushed her hair a hundred strokes a day. The gentleness of the man, the stories he told her in his dry, whispering voice, his steady, quiet, bony presence.

The girl stood up. She went to the window and stared out. In the light her hair seemed more auburn than brown. Her skin seemed to lose its pale, pasty look and took on the glow of ivory.

"It's hot in here," she said. "It's like a cage." She leaned out the open window and took a deep breath.

"Be careful now," the policeman said.

She looked at him over her shoulder and smiled. "Afraid I might pull a Moon?"

"What?"

"Nothing."

"Just come away."

"I can fly," she said. "My father taught me."

"Look, you're making me nervous there, girl," he said.

She pulled her head in and turned around. "Read to me."

Visitors got to Pullman by buying a fifty-cent round-trip ticket at the I. C. Central Depot at Michigan and Twelfth. The trip took forty minutes. The train ran along the edge of Lake Michigan, past Grant Park and swanky Prairie Avenue, where George Pullman had his mansion. Then the tracks turned west into open land, and fourteen miles out was Pullman Town. Passengers, Moon and Nick and Claire among them, saw the clock tower and the mighty Corliss engine from the train, broad green lawns and flowerbeds and beautiful Lake Vista.

The little man stepped down from the train and dusted the seat of his pants. "This sure beats the fair," he said. "This here's a real working man's town."

Moon looked around him. Beautiful. Real. He wished that Mae could see it. New and clean.

They walked south from the station, past the elegant Hotel Florence, the Arcade, the stables, the school, then cut over to Watt, past the home of Colonel Duane Doty, editor of the *Pullman Journal*, historian and manager of the town.

"It's a paradise," Moon said.

Claire gave him a wry smile. "Not exactly."

They turned right on Watt. The street was lined with neat, three-story red brick row houses. Curtains at the windows, flower-boxes.

"You live here?" Moon said.

"No. We're at the north end."

"We're just getting the grand tour," Nick said. "Mighty impressive."

"You might not think so if you lived here," Claire said.

"How's that?" Nick said. "Changing your tune?"

She shrugged. "Oh, I don't know. The company owns everything—the stores, the houses. They barge in whenever they want to 'inspect.'"

"Got to look after their interests."

"I suppose."

They looped around and turned north on Stephenson, passed the Market Place. Moon was elated. He didn't notice that the doors were shut tight, the windows small and high and shuttered. Maples and linden trees dappled the broad streets and camouflaged the mechanical regularity with which the houses had been laid out.

"This is us," Claire said, pointing. "Here." They turned up a trim walkway, and she produced her key.

Billy Barnes and his family—his wife, Cora, and one baby boy—lived in a row house, twenty feet wide, with two tiny bedrooms upstairs, a parlor, an eat-in kitchen. It was bigger than the tenements over on Fulton Street, but not nearly the equal of the fancy homes of the managers along Watt.

"Moon," Cora said when Claire introduced them. "I don't believe I've ever met a Moon."

"It's a family name," Moon said.

Claire—her real name was Alice—served tea in the parlor. The talk was polite. Then Billy Barnes came home. He was a big man with broad shoulders, dark, wiry hair, a walrus mustache. The discussion turned to the Pullman Palace Car Company, where Barnes worked as a skilled laborer.

"I hear George Pullman's got you folks under his thumb," the little man said.

Barnes set down his cup. "I wouldn't say that."

"You wouldn't, huh?"

"Have a cookie, Mr. Nickels," Cora said. The little man made her nervous.

"Any chance of a man getting work here?" Moon said.

Barnes scowled. "Not anymore there ain't."

"I heard the depression won't affect Chicago," Cora said. "Because of the fair."

"You heard wrong, missus," the little man said.

Barnes was wearing his Sunday suit, the one he wore to the Pullman Greenstone Church. His collar was starched and so white it seemed to glow in the gloom of the parlor.

"Yes, sir," the little man said, "this Pullman—"

"Mr. Nickels," Cora said, "would you like more tea?"

"You want to wise up," Nick said, holding out his cup. "Seize your destiny."

Barnes tugged at his collar. "Is that a fact?"

"It is," Nick said. He dumped in four or five heaping teaspoons of sugar. "Pullman don't have your best interests at heart."

"Nick." Claire was uncomfortable, and Cora kept passing the cookies.

"Look, if you got something to say . . ." Barnes twisted his neck, fighting the collar. "God *damn* this thing." He pulled it off with one quick jerk, and collar buttons bounced on the carpet.

"William!"

"He's fooling you boys," the little man said. He stuffed a cookie in his mouth and dusted crumbs off his greasy pants. "Hell, you ain't no better than Pullman's slaves."

"That ain't what you said before," Moon said.

"Am I talking to you?"

Barnes stood up.

"Boys," Claire said.

"Shut up," Nick told her. "Shut your goddamned mouth."

"Hey," Moon said, standing. "You ain't talking to her thataway, I don't give a damn."

"Well, that's the smartest thing you've said to date, son." Nick stood up and shucked out of his jacket. "Put 'em up, by Christ, if you don't give a damn."

"I won't have fist-fighting in my parlor," Cora said, but Moon had already swung at Nick, who ducked, and Cora, trying to separate them, took the blow square on the chin and fell in a heap on the parlor rug, at which time Billy Barnes stepped in, grabbed Nick by the collar with one hand and Jim Moon by the hair with the other, and threw them both out the door.

"And don't come back."

Nick picked himself up off the sidewalk. "What the hell's the matter with you, Moon?"

"You're aworking both sides of the street."

"Moonie, my boy, there are two sides, at least, to every question."

October 13, 1893
Dear Diary,

I fear I am some smit with this woman Claire, not wanting to be & so I believe is the Little Man Nick who I cannot seem to get shed of. He is forever there always talking & I am fearsome she believes his Bosh more than she ought. She is a Modern Girl & full of fun. Not as pretty as Mae & a little raw for a Lady—a Working Girl.

P.S. We went & seen Mr. Field's Store ystrday & it shows what I see now here is possible. There is Everything a man could want in Chicago.

"Look, colleen," the policeman said. "I'm not asking you to betray this man. But he's got family. Don't you think they got a right to know?"

The girl looked out the window. "See all them girls down there?"

The policeman was tired of talking. "I'll take your word on it," he said.

"Wanting things. Wanting. Know how I know?" She turned around and faced him. "I'm one of them girls."

"Well, I didn't think you was Mrs. John D. Rockefeller," he said.

She moved away from the window, and the light died from her hair. She crossed through the shadows and sat down on the bed. "Bet a man like you can't tell one kind of girl from another."

He looked at her. He'd looked at her before, of course, looked her over, looked into her eyes, searching for lies and weaknesses. But now, for the first time, he began to see her. She was not just thin but emaciated and pale, probably didn't eat regular and never had. Her teeth were stained. Her nails were chewed to the quick.

"You weren't born here, here in New York," he said.

"Nope."

Out of her depth. He knew it. Real New Yorkers had a certain style. The girls were corkers, bright as a dime, and they moved loose and easy, sure of themselves. This one, on the other hand, was nervous, stiff as a poker. Not that she'd ever admit it, not to him.

"Not from the old country?"

"Nein."

He crossed the room. "Not off the farm."

"Not hardly."

"What's your name, then?" he said.

"They named me Mary."

"Me mother's name."

"Like hell." She smoothed the pillowcase, propped it up behind her head, and leaned back. "They name all the orphan girls Mary. Mary Catherine, Mary Rose, Mary Margaret Magdalen."

He stared down at her.

"You've heard of me, then."

The policeman gave her a hard look. "Is it lying you are?"

"They call me Mamie, Molly, May, Maureen."

"That's Irish," he said.

"They call me a lot of things."

Homeless men were pouring into Chicago. They roamed the Loop and stood outside the fairgrounds, asking for work. A beggar approached Moon and the little man on State Street. "Spare a nickel?"

"Sorry, I'm looking for work myself," Moon told him.

"That's okay."

The fellow was starting to move on when a policeman nabbed him.

"Hey, wait a minute," Moon said. "He wasn't doing nothing."

The cop ignored him and hustled the tramp away.

"Did you see that?"

"Labor, Moon." The little man was pleased. "Just what the big boss needs. Desperation to grease the wheels of progress. And, of course, keep them wages down."

It was true. The girl couldn't read. Oh, they tried to teach her—good old St. Joe's. The nuns rapped her knuckles more than once for idleness, but the letters kept turning. An older girl who worked in the office took pity on her and read out her file: *Mary Elizabeth. Born Chicago, 1894. Mother unknown. Presumed deceased.* When she left, the sisters gave her a little cardboard box full of toiletries and underthings, took her picture, standing by the piano in the chilly reception hall.

Moon propped that picture up on the mantelpiece and studied her like a text: Five foot seven, pretty tall for a girl. Pale complexion and plain brown hair. Her face was heart-shaped—a broad forehead, a narrow chin. Eyes blue, as Moon's were, but darker, eyes that changed with the light.

She was too skinny, in her opinion, wished that she could put on twenty pounds. Her hair was thin and straight as a string, and the only thing she liked about herself was the name she had chosen.

Grimes. It suited her. That was what she remembered. On the

big iron stoves, on the windowsills, in the water closet near the base of the toilet where the water seeped out, mixed with piss, and dug into the wooden planking, turning it slimy black.

"Grimes," said Sister John of the Cross, the matron. "An odd choice."

"It was my mother's maiden name."

Sister looked up from the papers on her desk, her eyes the gray of winter rain. "I don't think so, dear."

The girl invented relatives—uncles, cousins, multitudes named Grimes.

"All right, then," Sister said. "I don't suppose it matters very much."

"As blessed as the fair has been with clement weather," Moon read in the morning paper, "the month of October has crowned it with radiant glory." The waitress in the greasy spoon where Moon was taking his breakfast poured him another cup of wicked black coffee.

"The air is crisp," Moon read, "lending exhilaration to exertion, and the azure of a clear sky contends playfully with that of Lake Michigan itself. The White City"—Moon wet his thumb and turned the page—"is brilliant beneath a swirl of flags and colorful banners, shining like an opulent jewel as it nears its closing day."

"Hear the news?" The little man burst through the door with an extra edition of the *Tribune*. "'Mayor Harrison Shot to Death in His Home.'"

Moon was so lost in playful azure, it took him a moment to comprehend.

"Our Carter." The little man shook his head in despair. "Gone but not forgotten." He slipped into the booth across from Moon. "Some fella unhappy about his situation, I reckon." He started to read. "Ah, yes, 'Disgruntled,' says here." He took a sip from Moon's cup. "Disaffected. My, my. Things is tough all over."

The policeman sat down on the bed beside the girl. "How come you don't like me, then?" he said.

"I like you."

"Oh, sure."

"What do you care whether I like you or not?"

The policeman took her hand. "I'm not trying to hurt you here, you know."

She looked into his eyes. They were pale and misty. Irish eyes.

"You know, you can trust me," he said. He kissed her.

"Oh, that kind of like," she said.

He studied her face. "Tell me, Mary—if that's your name— what's this old man to you?"

She smelled a little like fresh-cut bluegrass underneath the sweat, a summertime smell. He ran his fingertip down her neck, and she turned and looked him straight in the eye.

"Didn't you ever get tired, feel like you just wanted to lean up against somebody?"

The policeman considered. "I suppose."

"People get dead tired. That ain't a crime."

The policeman lay back, settled a pillow under his head. The sheets were soft and carried the scent of her.

"See?" She stretched out beside him. "You know how it is."

In deference to the death of the mayor, the fair closed quietly. Mae Moon back in Iowa read about it in the Winterset paper. Final-day festivities were canceled, and the fabulous World's Columbian Exposition came to an end.

The weather turned cold. The dancers and pitchmen, the waiters and aborigines went home, the cooks and the draymen, the entrepreneurs. The exhibits were dismantled, the statues crated and hauled away, the banners pulled down. Overnight it was gone, that happy nowhere. What was there now but ordinary life?

Moon did not return to Iowa, and Mae grew restless. She had been wrong, perhaps, too conventional. To keep herself busy, she turned the bed, mended sheets, whitewashed the parlor, laundered the curtains and washed and ironed her husband's two blue work shirts and replaced three missing buttons. Even old and scarred as he was, she considered Moon handsome. She pictured him at the table, loading sugar into his coffee and stirring it in quick half-swirls. The Whitman book or the newspaper would be open at his elbow. She wished he were there to read to her now. Anything would be pleasant to hear. Jimmy.

The policeman unfastened the tiny pearl buttons of the girl's blue cotton dress as though he'd done it a hundred times before. "Pretty," he said.

Her skin was damp, white, the fur between her legs a rich sable brown. She didn't make any effort to stop him. "You're taking this easy enough," he said.

"Want me to kick and bite?"

"Maybe. A little."

"Too darn hot."

A small struggle might be a good thing, the policeman thought, just to keep the lines drawn. On the other hand, they both knew how the game was played. He took off his shirt and unbuttoned his trousers. Why not? All the boys at the station took a little bit for protection. Not exactly pristine goods, so what harm would it do?

"You'll not tell on me," he said.

"Depends on how good you are."

The whaleback steamer had quit running from midtown to the pier. The Ferris wheel hung motionless against the sky. The fair was over, but Moon could not go home. Every time he pictured himself returning, a failed man squirming beneath forgiveness, he found another reason to stay in Chicago. He missed them, of course, Mae and the boy, and tried to write more than once, but the words wouldn't come. It wasn't only the money he had lost. It was something deeper, some energy. The dream had been there. He had seen it, walked along the paths of a bright new world. He had not been mistaken—that would have been easy. Just bamboozled. The magic had vanished, not like a dream in an instant, leaving belief intact, but in one disappointment after another. How could he explain to her how it had gone?

The girl nestled close and licked the policeman's ear. "Who's the first girl you ever kissed?"

"You." He shook his head. "That tickles."

"No, seriously."

He leaned over and stared into her eyes. "I'm absolutely and totally dead serious," he said. "Never more so, girl, believe me."

She smiled. "Let's take our time."

The policeman took a silver watch out of his pants pocket and handed it to her. "You be the timekeeper, then."

She dangled the watch on its chain, forcing it into lazy circles. "So, who was she?"

"The first one? Lizzie Burke. She was a Protestant," he said. "Older than me. My brother Rowan swore that I'd go to hell."

"You could yet."

"I figured it might be worth it."

"Was she pretty?"

The policeman stretched out on the bed and smiled. "She had remarkable hair," he said. "Pale, pale, all braided up." He twisted his fingers together to show how it was. "And once I gave her a penny to untie the blue ribbons she wore and shake her hair out over my belly."

The girl sat up and unpinned her hair, shook it lightly over his chest.

"It still affects me."

The people in town had begun to talk—another woman, they said. Mae Moon's neighbors pitied her. "Gone to the fair," they said—the way they said it. "The Vanity Fair." They ridiculed her loyalty, her love, and sometimes she couldn't help but feel that their scorn was justified. Moon's conduct was unforgivable.

· · ·

The policeman nuzzled his face against the girl's neck and kissed her. She didn't resist. "All right?" he said. He stroked her thigh. "So, is it time or no?"

She was so silent he thought for a moment she might be drifting to sleep.

"I'm not wanting to hurt you, you know," he said.

He eased himself on top of her. The girl did not respond. He stroked her hair, kissed her again, but she didn't move a muscle, nothing, not the least response.

"Damn it," he said.

"What?"

Was this lovemaking or force or what was it at all? He rolled off. "You can't make anything simple, can you?"

Mae was stoic, preoccupied with the duties of motherhood. Little Win was a handful. He looked like his father. There was always something—laundry, marketing—to do. She tried not to keep close track of the days, but when the first light snow fell, her patience gave out. The fire burned low, and frost took the windows. Evening came early, and anger began to emerge from her longing and shame.

"He has no right," she said. She tucked her son in the cradle and rocked it furiously. "Moon has responsibilities."

The policeman felt like a fool. "You're the most aggravating girl I've ever known," he said.

She nestled against him, the watch in her hand. "I thought we was doing pretty good there for a while."

Shadows fell from the bare cottonwood trees. Mrs. Moon curled up in the double bed and dreamed of her husband's angular body, the scent of him. They didn't know her Jimmy. He had great vision. She had always believed so. Intellectual passion. He was a seeker. How could simple farm people understand? Another woman indeed. Ridiculous. She woke at dawn and dressed herself and the baby. Leaving Winslow in the care of a neighbor, Mrs. Ross, she bought a railway ticket for Chicago.

The girl and the policeman stared up at the ceiling.

"Mad?"

"No, I guess not," he said.

"It's just so hot."

He closed his eyes. "I had the chicken pox when I was eight," he said absently. "It was summer, like now, hot. And I was shut up in the back bedroom, my parents' bedroom, the only room in the house with a door and a lock on it. The only real *room*, as far as that went. Had a bed like this one, a double, all jingly. The sheets got so hot my mother used to fan me." He closed his eyes, seining for details. "The fan was paper, shaped like a broad leaf, and it said, 'Dunn's Funeral Home. The wise man knows it is never too soon to prepare.'"

"Cheerful thought," the girl said.

"The urge to scratch was absolutely fierce. I wanted to claw the hide right off my bones."

"I see you didn't."

He opened his eyes and smiled. "My mother tied my wrists to the bedposts—a 'homey crucifixion,' Rowan called it. And wasn't he skinned alive for that observation."

The policeman seemed to be talking to himself.

"And it was just darkness, you know, and the sounds of the other boys outside, going on with their games, laughing, already forgetting about me. Sure, I thought I would die in that room. Shrivel up like the dead rats we found sometimes, my brothers and me, curled up beside the trash bins where the landlord put out the poison. I knew early what happens to the dead. How the lips pull back and the toes curl. The skin goes white as a nun's veil."

The girl turned away.

"Oh, Christ, I'm sorry," he said.

She started to whimper.

"What?" He sat up. "What is it?"

96

"Nothing."

He touched her shoulder. "You couldn't have cared. Mary. About an old man?"

She started to sob.

"Don't, darling, no. Hush." He took her in his arms. "None of us are worth a woman's tears."

The fountains in the White City were still. Frost had formed on the steel girders of the buildings, and newspapers blew down the walkways. The fair, just as the little man had claimed, was an illusion. For Chicago, it had only postponed the depression, which was nationwide, brought on in part by overexpansion and mismanagement in the railroad industry. As early as June, George Pullman had told the public to prepare for "hard times." Now the industry had a three-year supply of railroad cars on hand. Wages were cut. Pullman had closed his Detroit plant and replaced the popular Pullman manager, H. H. Sessions, with a less understanding man. A piecework system was adopted, and just as the little man had predicted, Pullman began acquiring contracts at a loss.

"How'd you get to be a cop?"

"Oh, that's a long story," he said.

"We got time."

"Well, let's see." The policeman settled back and cupped his hands behind his head. "Big Bill Nolan put me wise."

"Owns the Shamrock."

"Right. I was a runner, carrying paper bags from place to place. 'Never look inside,' says he."

"But you did."

"Sure. And weren't they full of lovely green money."

The Shamrock was a hole in the wall with a private room in the back. There was a long mahogany bar, Nolan's pride and joy, an elaborate backbar with the name of the place etched in the beveled mirror. Nolan filled the fancy-label bottles with cheap stuff, and the free lunch was skimpy—stale crackers and rat-trap cheese—except for certain persons, who were allowed to partake of the better eats in the back. Card games there, high stakes, with Doyle Maguire and Danny Shaw always the biggest winners.

"When I saw that room, I says to myself, 'Michael, you're home.' Not that it was swank. Just cozy-like."

Mrs. Moon, tired and anxious, arrived in Chicago and took a room in a boarding house recommended to her by a little man she met outside Union Station. Conveniently, it was right near the fairgrounds.

"There was a big round table," the policeman said, "and I used to sit underneath that table sometimes—I was nine or ten—pretending to sleep and reading the cards for Doyle. I signaled by pulling his pants cuff. My initials are still there, I'll bet, cut underneath with the penknife Big Bill gave me. He'd murder me if he knew I carved up his table."

"I'll never tell."

"The walls were painted green, I remember, pale—puke green, Nolan called it—and the back door opened onto an alley, blind at the one end, or I should say, bound by a high brick wall. Which I, being young and big for my age, could scale, but Bill and the other men could not. My job, when the law came around, was to scurry up the wall and sit on top. Then just when the cops came out the back door, I'd scramble down the other side, making all the racket I could, see."

The girl smiled.

"They'd think the whole gang had gone my way, over the wall. Course, Bill and them took off in the other direction, stuffing money in their pockets and running for dear life."

The policeman sat up and rolled himself a cigarette. "Good times," he said.

"Sounds like."

"I grew up in that back room."

"And the ones upstairs."

He brushed her nose with the tip of his thumb. "You mind your own business."

The policeman lit the cigarette and handed it to the girl. "I learned a couple of tricks from Nolan—the pigeon drop, the cap game. Went on the stroll with Doyle a couple of times. But the rackets are not for boys like me."

"Too smart," she said.

The policeman shrugged. "I don't know. Bill finally wised me up—'Your kind ends up cold meat,' says he. He was a world-beater, old Billy."

"What did he mean by 'your kind'?"

"I don't know."

"Softhearted."

"Softheaded, more like," he said. "Told me to join the force, where I could be 'useful.'"

The girl took a drag and passed back the cigarette. "Aren't there any German cops? Bohemians, Polish, Chinamen cops?"

He shook his head. "No, we're all of us Irish."

"Like to keep things in the family, I guess."

"Precisely. Share the wealth."

The girl smiled. "What did your father think?"

"Long gone by then."

"Sorry."

"Don't be. He died of the drink."

"That's tough," she said.

"It happens. Rowan was destroyed, but I was older. I still remembered the way he was."

He offered her the cigarette. She shook her head. He stubbed it out on the floor. "I was all times look for work after that. And found none. At least, nothing outside of Nolan's circle. It's pissing in the wind you were, looking to find some other kind of life."

"Like what?"

"I don't know. Factory work, shopkeeper."

"No money in honor," the girl said.

"Amen to that."

Homeless men huddled in doorways, brooding. They rubbed their hands together over an open fire. They talked about the promise that had brought them to Chicago and how the bottom had shifted from under their feet.

The girl turned toward the policeman. "It's time."

"Are you serious?"

She nodded.

He stroked her cheek. "Truly," he said, "I'll not hurt you."

"I know."

He climbed on top. "I'm a little bit . . ."

"Stop fussing," she said.

The girl took his cock in her hand and stroked it, rubbed her thumb over the tip and guided it inside. "There, Mr. Mike the Cop, how's that now?"

"All right," he said.

The bed began to rock. The springs sighed. They rolled over, the girl on top, her hair tenting his face, then back over again. She reached above her head and grabbed hold of the bedframe.

"All right?" he said.

She looked into his eyes. There was kindness there, guarded, not often exercised, perhaps, but it was real. She let go of the bars and wrapped her legs around his waist and felt a hollow ache in the pit of her stomach pulling him in.

"I'm afraid I didn't make myself clear when we met at the station," Mae said. "I'm a married woman."

"Just a walk." The little man flashed her a grin. "Ain't you tired of being cooped up all day?"

They were talking in the parlor of the boarding house where Mae had taken a room. "I have felt a little housebound since I arrived," she said.

The little man tipped his derby hat and offered his arm. "C'mon then, Mrs. Mae Moon. Let's get the stink blowed off."

Mae and the little man left the house and walked toward the lake. The evening was clear and a scattering of stars was visible.

"Moon," the little man said. "Interesting name."

She touched his arm eagerly. "Do you know anyone else by that name?" She blushed a little. "I'm looking for someone."

"Brother?"

Mae smiled shyly. "No. Just somebody I misjudged."

"Some fella you didn't know very well," Nick prompted.

"I guess not. But someone I want to get to know better."

The little man squinted, rubbed his chin. "Moon, Moon. Nope. Can't say as I do."

"I'd be willing to pay for information."

The little man smiled in the darkness. "Money?"

Mae was confused. "Why, yes."

"See, there's all kinds of ways a person can pay."

They walked on in silence, enjoying the air, listening to the whisper along the breakwaters. Farther north, the city glowed on the shore.

"You know," Nick said, "you and me. Meeting up at the train station like that. Some folks might call that an accident."

"Wasn't it? Coincidence?"

"Yes and no," he said. "It's a big old world, but she holds together."

"I'm not sure I understand."

"Bits and pieces, floating around. Dead leaves in a crick." He stirred the air with his fingertips. "But once things come together, *coincide* . . ." He interlaced his fingers, making a cage of his hands. "That's destiny. The old kismet."

"Well," she said, "you're a philosophical man."

"I enjoy a good wrangle."

"My father used to say that a man carries his fate within him."

"Well, he was right. Take you, for instance."

She smiled. "I hardly think I have a *fate*."

"No, you're the key to the whole shebang," he said. "See, here's the thing. You was *moved* to come. Had some feelings for this 'somebody' fella you was just now talking about. Course, from my point of view, that's the fly in the ointment."

Mae was puzzled.

"Never mind," he said.

They walked on, arm in arm. The little man could be quite debonair. "So how's Chicago treating you?" he said. "Having fun?"

"I'm a bit overwhelmed, I guess."

The little man looked around him. "The boss city of the universe."

Mae smiled. "It *is* beautiful."

The little man pulled on his earlobe. "And, madam, so are you."

Two men came out of nowhere. One carried a horse blanket, not neatly folded over his arm but lifted and stretched in front of him like a moving wall, and before Mae could run or even cry out, he had thrown the blanket over her head and wrapped his arms around her.

She struggled. She felt herself being lifted off her feet, slung over his shoulder. The blanket tightened. She couldn't see. It smelled of some sort of chemical, and she couldn't catch her breath. The man was running. A door opened.

"Let me go!"

It was useless to fight, but she kicked and squirmed. Male voices were arguing—"Keep her quiet." She was placed in a carriage, pushed to the floor. She tried to get up and twisted her knee, and somebody shoved her down. "Behave yourself."

The horses must have been nervous. The carriage rolled back and then suddenly started forward, moving fast. She heard the crack of a whip.

They took a corner, left, and then another. Mae was frantic, so tightly bound she could hardly breathe. The little man must have been sitting above her. Somebody's boots were resting on her hip.

"Stop wiggling," he told her. He gave her a kick.

She struggled. He kicked her again. "Stick with me, girl," he said, "and I'll have you farting through silk 'fore morning."

Moon, beneath the river, swirled in the current, felt a gentle rocking, ceased to dream. A garbage scow was moving up the river, pushing, urging. Water surged around him. His boots slipped off. The fabric of his coat began to tear away, and rotting, unshriven, Moon began to simmer.

The carriage rolled through the darkness. Mae, underneath the blanket, sensed a change: other carriages, other sounds mingling with the steady clip of the horses' hooves. They slowed frequently. Once they came to a halt and started again. There were many turns. Finally the carriage stopped.

She heard whispering, a subdued argument. Then the little man was pulling her out. "Get her feet," he told someone, and rough invisible hands grabbed hold of her ankles. She was terrified now. She struggled, kicking, trying to twist free.

"Regular wildcat." Somebody laughed.

The air was cold, then warmer. She was inside some sort of building. The captors set her on her feet, and looking down, she could see a patch of red Oriental carpet. She heard footsteps approaching, quick, hard taps, perhaps down a staircase.

"Here she is, safe and sound."

A pair of black leather boots became visible. She heard the sound of coins changing hands, and the blanket was lifted just enough to allow two puffy, well-manicured hands to run over her hips.

"As promised," the little man said.

"Tell me about yourself and the old man," the policeman said. "He ever do this to you?"

"He was a union man."

The policeman burst out laughing. "By Christ, you're a corker, girl. What's that got to do with anything?"

"You said, 'Tell me about him.'"

"No, no, I mean the *man*. Why'd he do it?" he said. "Money troubles? Love?"

"You think that's strange?"

"To Brodie off a ferry boat and leave a girl as accommodating as you?" He brushed her hair back with his hand and kissed her forehead. "I do indeed."

She moved a little closer. "Did you ever see one of those moving picture wheels?"

"A zoetrope?"

"You look through these little slits, and you see a man walking."

"Or the devil. What about them?"

She flipped her pillow, searching for the cool spot underneath. "He's not really moving, that little man."

"It's an illusion."

"After a while, you figure out it's just an endless circle. The same thing over and over."

The policeman considered. "So your man was wore out, was he? Tired of going in circles."

"Him and me both."

The policeman frowned.

"What?" she said.

"I don't know. A man that old. His worries should be over. Nothing to do but sit by the fire and smoke his pipe. You know what I mean," he said. "He should be going straight, not crooked, into a peaceful old age."

"Peace," she said.

The policeman resettled his hands behind his head. "Grief and despair are for a man in his prime, a man mixed up in things."

"Things?"

"This union business. Was there money involved?"

"How do you mean?"

"Money," he said. "The root of all evil, the cause of murder and mayhem. Tell me, Maureen, was your man in the rackets?"

She kissed him and twisted a curl into his stiff red hair. "He had some friends."

"In Jersey?"

"Could be."

He leaned over close. "Where's the money?"

She smiled. "I thought we were talking about old age."

"Money adds interest to any discussion," he said.

"Well, he didn't have no money. Not the kind you're talking about."

"Right."

The policeman swung his legs over the edge of the bed. Stubborn. He stood up and ran his fingers through his hair. "He must have had a wallet, a sock full of coins?" he said.

"Nope."

"Maybe he had it and lost it. Maybe he thought somebody might come looking. Gave it to you for safekeeping, then panicked and did himself in."

The girl fell silent, picked at her nails.

"It's no good to you, you know," he said.

She didn't respond.

"But *me*." He looked around for his trousers. "That loot would be the making of me."

He found his pants on the floor and stepped into them, buttoning up. "I'd get the copper then sure."

"What's that?" she said.

"A promotion."

"You're a man with ambitions, then. Mother will be so pleased."

The room in which Mae found herself was small but well-furnished, with a brass bed and a walnut washstand, a writing table, and an easy chair. The room was comfortable, even pretty, in a way. The lamp was turned low and projected a soft play of shadows on the walls.

She had been carried in and dumped on the bed by a young

man in work clothes who shut the door behind him when he left. She tried it immediately, of course. It was locked. The room had only one window, and it was nailed shut. But it might be possible, she thought, to break the glass and somehow . . . What? Jump? The window opened onto an air shaft, but it was three floors to the ground, and from what she could see, there was no way out to the street at the bottom.

Another window faced hers from across the way. Would it be possible to bridge the air shaft? Maybe with a railing from the bed? Crawl across and escape. But into what?

She stared across. Lace curtains, the same pattern that adorned her window, a faint light beyond them, and then—was that a woman's form? Mae tapped on her window. She took the lamp from the table and moved it back and forth to signal, but if there was anyone there, she failed to respond.

"I'm a Catholic," the policeman said.

"Well, bully for you."

"Don't you know his soul will go to hell?"

She smiled.

"It's no joke, Maureen. The man's in peril."

"He didn't want to be found," she said.

"That's immaterial now." He picked up his shirt and punched his arms through the sleeves. "You tell me everything, and the man can rest in peace."

The girl began to laugh.

"What's so damned comical?"

"You are. Talking about peace."

"You'll not laugh at the Holy Catholic Church."

"Ha, ha, ha."

He grabbed her by the hair and gave her a slap and she slapped him back. "So," he said, "you won't be satisfied."

"Solidarity," the little man said. He had waited for Billy Barnes in an alleyway near the Pullman works and hooked him in with his bamboo cane when he passed. "Ain't no one worker can stand alone."

"You're a son of a bitch," Barnes said, "but, by God, you're right."

"Put her there."

The sky was a pewter gray. A slushy snow fell.

"Happens I have a little hair of the dog," Nick said. "Dutch courage. I hear it's mighty dry out here in the sticks."

"That it is."

"You're a drinking man."

"I am," said Barnes.

"Well, then."

The men huddled against a wall, out of the wind, and drank, and the little man agreed with whatever Barnes said. There was nothing at stake. No money. Nothing immediate. But sometimes, for Nick, just conning an honest man was reward enough.

"Mealy-mouthed little son of a bitch," Barnes said, meaning Pullman. "I could break him in half."

The little man leaned in close. "Why don't you, then?"

The policeman pushed the girl back down on the bed. "Get dressed," he said. He had wasted too much time with her already, let himself get too involved.

The girl curled up like a child.

"Don't go sniveling now."

She refused to answer him.

"Come, let's call it a draw."

Pity nudged him, but pity or no, she couldn't be let to insult Holy Mother Church.

"Come on, girl," he said. "I thought you liked me there for a little."

She looked up at him then. "What I like—"

"Come and get dressed."

"—don't have much to do with anything, does it?"

The policeman stood over her, hiking up his suspenders.

"Tell me about your man's union business. Was he an organizer or what?"

The girl sat up and shrugged. "I don't know. There was some kind of strike. Him and this friend—"

"He had a friend, then?"

"Yeah, someone he met in that white city."

"And you don't know the name of that man either, I suppose."

She shook her head.

"Striking, were they?"

She nodded.

"Strikes are bad things."

"Why?"

He thought it over. "Because they disturb the status quo," he said. "Do you know what that is?"

"Them that's got is them that get."

He considered. "Yeah, I suppose."

She sat on the bed and watched him button his shirt, the smooth white barrel chest disappearing beneath the dingy linen. "Just folks wanting to be treated right is all."

On December 9, a few Pullman steamfitters and blacksmiths led a halfhearted strike, and the next day a letter appeared in the *Chicago Times*, signed "Employees":

> Well-known it is that George Pullman had things misrepresented to him. Mr. Pullman is a fine fellow and what he wants is fine fellows to work for him. . . . Give Mr. Sessions charge of us and the workers will go smoothly. He is the boy who we can help to estimate low enough to catch every car order in the market, and when we bid too low we will work for lower wages to help him, but we can't help the present management. No, not a bit of it.

The strike lasted only a few days. At first, Barnes, one of the strikers, refused to return to his job, but threatened with the blacklist he gave in.

. . .

December 15, 1893

Dear Diary,

We are camping—the little man & me—I now call him Nick & sometimes Red—in the Manufactures Building at the fairgrounds. There are alots of other men here too looking for work—or just waiting. Sickness is among us—Smallpox & Typhoid Fever. None of the men have got homes & their Wives & Families have mostly forgot about them, they believe, as I'm sure has my own.

The little man threw a piece of wooden railing on the fire. When the weather turned cold, the homeless men had begun to dismantle the interior of the building, burning whatever would burn to keep themselves warm.

"God damn Cleveland," somebody said. "God damn the bosses."

"Damn yourself," the little man said. "Don't you know that you are a moral failure? It's in all the papers. Read for yourselves. They's opportunities. This here's the *land* of opportunity, rubes."

There was grumbling at first from the men around the fire, then a long silence—just the spit and crackle of the flames. The man who had spoken hung his head. "I reckon you're right," he said.

"No." This from Jim Moon.

"I'm no good," the man said. "And I know it."

"No."

"What do you know about it, Moon?" the little man said. "You just fell off the turnip wagon your own self."

"I know a man wants work ain't to blame if there ain't no work to be had."

"Moon, you're talking like an anarchist."

Jim Moon and T. J. Nickels dined with the Barnes family on Christmas Day, down in Pullman. It was a modest meal.

"Stewed chicken."

"William, please."

"On Christmas Day."

"Wonder what old George Pullman is having?" Nick said. "Pass me them peas."

Thanks to Claire, matters had long since been patched up between her brother and Jim Moon. Nick, for some strange reason, had always been welcome.

"Wonder if it's oysters in his stuffing," Nick said. "Or them yeller raisins. Ever have them?"

"That's enough," Moon said. He brought his fist down hard on the table. "Eat and be happy you got it."

Billy folded his napkin and pushed back from the table. "No, he's right. Damned Pullman."

"What's the difference," Nick said, "being a wage slave, being a peasant back in the old country?"

"There's a world of difference," Claire said hotly.

"You're still under somebody's boot," Nick said.

"Gentlemen." Cora rose from her place at the foot of the table. She was wearing her black taffeta with the white lace collar, her best, and her hair had been braided in an intricate crisscross, like a coronet. No one would say she was beautiful, but in the candlelight, standing her ground, she had something—courage, integrity—that the men respected.

"This is our Savior's birthday," she said.

The men studied their plates.

"And I have a very nice rice pudding cooling in the pantry." She looked to her right. "Mr. Moon?"

"That sounds real good," he said.

A red kimono lay on the bed. Mae had never worn anything so fancy. The wardrobe contained a number of corsets, stockings, colorful frocks. Her own plain blue cotton dress seemed hopelessly drab next to the bright silks and satins. She picked up a shirtwaist and rubbed the glossy fabric against her cheek.

A young man knocked on the door, opened it, and leaned in.

An older woman, heavily made up, stood behind him. He stepped aside and the woman poked her head through the doorway. "Visitor!"

"I'd like to stay," the policeman said.

The girl said nothing.

"But I been cooping long enough." He smiled.

She refused to look at him.

"The sarge'll be after me."

He took his coat from the chair and struggled into it. "Too warm for this rig," he said.

It was impossible to read her expression. Anger, contempt, sorrow, betrayal? He hadn't meant to hurt her.

He fastened a few buttons, then quit. "Maybe I'll just let the breeze blow through." He picked up his cap from the table and settled it on his head. "Leatherhead," he said, pointing to the cap.

The girl had still not spoken. He looked at her critically. "Now don't go getting any ideas," he said.

"About what?"

She hadn't bothered to button her dress, and the policeman could see a curve of milky white flesh and the hollow of her collarbone and the soft rounded angle of her shoulder. Her hair was down, coiled over her breasts. Something caught and twisted inside him.

"Cover up," he said.

"Why?"

"Because I said so."

"I don't want you wearing these buttons out."

In two strides he was across the room. He grabbed a handful of blue cotton dress and hauled her upright. "Look," he said. "It just happened. You wanted it too, missy. Besides, this isn't anything new for you."

The girl refused to respond.

"You'll not tell anyone either," he said.

She ignored him.

"No one would believe you if you did."

The girl hung limp from his hands, and that made him angry. "No one cares what happens to you," he said.

"A living monument," the little man said. He and Moon were headed for the train.

"You're drunk."

"To the culture, philanthropy, enterprise, and business capacity of—"

"George Pullman," Moon said. He kicked a stone on the walkway.

The rigid orderliness of the town and the prominence of the factory had begun to seem confining. It was the old question of cost again. There was no public saloon in Pullman Town. Only the high muckety-mucks were welcome at the bar in the Hotel Florence. Everything was regulated, evaluated, controlled. The gridwork of the streets and the boxy houses now seemed to Moon like a kind of prison.

"Prison?" the little man said. "Hell's fire. This is utopia, Moon. And Pullman? The man's a genius. He's like a goddamned father to these folks."

"Pullman Town. It's just like being owned."

"'Future generations will bless his memory.'"

"How's that?"

"I'm quoting the *Times*," the little man said. "You wouldn't argue with the *Times*."

"You got an old paper."

Part Two

MOON SANK like a stone and failed to rise, his pockets being full of broken staff. Near the bottom his jacket caught on an angle of jagged scrap iron, which detained him, held him swaying in the muddy current and, gradually, ceasing to be Moon. Thus snagged, eluding both the gaff man and the net, he contemplated, remembered, found his ultimate purpose and promptly forgot it, had his vision, danced his lonely jig. Three days later, a scow, churning up the river, shook him loose from this temporary mooring and sent him weaving upward toward the light.

"Name?"
  "Jim Moon."
  "Ever work stock before?"
  "No."
  "Sorry, fella. Next!"

"Excuse me. My name's Moon."
  "Nothing today."
  "I'm willing to do anything," Moon said.
  "You speak English?"
  "Yes, sir."
  "*Nothing today.*"

May 1, 1894
Dear Diary,
  The Depression continues. Some of us beg & some steal. Claire

says things are bad at Pullman too. She has been laid off from the Embroidering Department due to the Panic. Mr. Pullman will not reduce the rents tho wages have been cut considerable & the Company deducts expenses also so that her Brother has brought home only four dollars & 63 cent for the last half of April & the Foremen's wages are not reduced.

The guard at the gate lifted his hands, palms out, waving them off. "Fair's over, buddy."

"That a fact?"

"Has been for six months."

The little man held Claire's hand and fixed the guard with his dark, flickering eyes. "We just want to take a stroll," he said.

Jim Moon looked around him. A local company had been engaged to remove the buildings at a rate of five cents per hundredweight, beginning with the state and foreign buildings to the north. Moon could see horses and drays in the distance, almost transparent and moving like ghosts through the dust.

The guard hesitated, squinting in the pale sunlight.

"Just looking around," the little man said quietly. "Ain't gonna hurt anything."

All around them the city seemed to slow. The birds fell silent. The horses stopped and shook their harness. The White City brooded beside the lake.

"You one of them agitators?" the guard said.

"You can trust me."

The guard hesitated, then opened the gate.

"Now that's a good fella," the little man said.

They passed through. Claire was impressed. "You certainly have a way about you," she said.

"He's a friend of mine."

"I heard that no one was allowed inside the gates. Didn't you, Mr. Moon?"

The little man smiled. "The boys, the campers, Moon and me,

get in over the fence, under the wire. They's dozens of holes, ways and ways. Squirm in and out like sewer rats. The whole damn fair's infested—pardon my French. But a lady"—he bowed to Claire—"well, now, that wouldn't be right."

They strolled toward the basin, watching the terns wheel over the water. The Court of Honor remained, the walkways, the bridges and statues, but everything had a shabby, abandoned look. The buildings were chipped like old crockery.

"She's looking a little tired," Nick said.

"It's still very beautiful, though." Claire looked around her. "If I didn't know better, I'd think I was somewhere in Europe."

"Or back in them Roman times."

"It's supposed to be new," Moon said. "The future."

"Sometimes the future scares me," she said. "Everything's changing so fast. Funny. I think of myself as a modern woman."

Moon tried to offer some comfort, but Nick nudged him out of the way.

"I wish I could live *here*," she said.

"Why not?" the little man said. "It's got everything—or did. Police, fire department, sanitation crew, water system, transportation."

"It seems safe," she said. "It's like a still point. We're just on the verge, not really in the past or in the future."

She turned to Nick. "What will happen to it now? The buildings, I mean."

"Burnham don't know whether to leave it, raze it, or burn it down," he said. "What do you do with a worn-out dream anyhow?"

For Jim Moon's part, he would have kept every building intact, every statue in its place, every flower in bloom, every electric light bulb twinkling. "But that can't be, can it?" Moon said.

"Nope. She's got to go."

They looked back at the Administration Building, Claire's favorite. A chilly, thin sunlight spilled over the dome. Claire looked up, admiring the allegorical statues. "Earth, Air, Fire, and Water."

"Like the four points of a compass," Moon said.

"Like angels at the four corners of the earth."

"In their uncontrolled and in their *civilized* state," the little man said. "Haw, haw. That's a hot one." He tugged at his collar.

"But that's what civilization is," Claire said. "Control. And 'harnessing nature.'"

"Ever see fire?"

Moon bristled. "Don't you be showing her nothing."

"Sir, you offend me deeply. I wouldn't dream of displaying my hide to a lady." The little man bowed. "Besides, tempus fugit."

"How's that?"

"I have urgent bidness. Some gentlemen—you don't know 'em, bidnessmen—are meeting me here, over at the Electricity Building."

"So you're a businessman."

"Sure."

"Don't surprise me a bit," Moon said.

"Well, time and tide." The little man tipped his derby. "Madam. Oops, I mean *Miss* Barnes." He turned to Moon. "Moonie, take care of my girl."

Claire was offended. "I'm sure, Mr. Nickels, that I can manage to take care of myself."

"Now that's where you're wrong, missy," Nick said. "She's one tough old town."

He walked away, twirling his cane, his frayed coattails swaying. His shoes were too big for his feet, worn brogans with broken laces that trailed along behind him as he walked.

"Struts like a crow," Moon said.

"Who is he, anyway?"

"You'd know better than me," Moon said.

"What's that supposed to mean?"

"He tells me he's your intended."

"He is not."

Claire wore the star-shaped garnet pin at her throat. "Who give you that, then?" Moon said. "Huh? He give it to you? Nick?"

"What if he did?"

Moon shrugged. "Yeah, I guess."

"I don't belong to you."

She walked away, and Moon rushed after her.

"I don't belong to anyone," she said.

Moon offered his arm, but she refused him. She wouldn't speak, and Moon was miserable. He tagged along as she crossed a footbridge, still not speaking, stopped to admire a statue. When she thought he had learned his lesson, she smiled. "Apology accepted," she said.

They walked east, toward the lake. The city seemed watery and insubstantial. The buildings were dingy with coal smoke, and the veneer of staff had begun to crack and warp, falling away in places from the dark iron skeletons underneath.

"Do they really want to burn it down?" Moon said, looking around him. "Daniel Burnham and them."

"Rather than see it deteriorate," she said.

Moon glanced away. "I don't believe I could stand to see that," he said.

"Oh, Mr. Moon, it's just a model. Like a sketch."

"It's not real."

"Well, no."

"It is, though."

Moon stooped and picked up a piece of broken staff, turned it end to end in his hands, then skipped it across the water.

"That doesn't mean it isn't beautiful," Claire said. "Just because it won't last."

She was wearing the white eyelet blouse, Moon's favorite, and a dark green cotton skirt. She had removed her hat, and the wind off the lake teased her pale blond hair.

"It's a symbol," she said. "It's a promise. This is what the future could be like."

"You think so?"

"Don't you?"

Moon was silent.

"Anyway, why brood? It's all ours now. At least for the moment."

Moon smiled. "It is, isn't it?"

She ran ahead of him, twirled in the sunlight, and raised both slender arms above her head.

"It's spring," she said, returning to Moon. "Doesn't that make you happy?" She took both of his hands in hers and looked up at him, teasing. "I don't belong to him either."

"You one of them modern women?" Moon said.

"Yes, as a matter of fact."

"Wanting to vote?"

"Why shouldn't I?"

He held her hand, amazed at the delicate structure of what he imagined were pure white bones beneath the skin. "Would you vote for me?"

She smiled at him. "That all depends."

"On what?"

"I'd have to get to know you better," she said.

They walked on. "Tell me about yourself," she said. "Nick talks so much I haven't gotten to know you hardly at all."

"Nothing to tell," Moon said.

She turned toward him, flirting openly. "I don't believe that for one minute," she said. She leaned toward him confidentially. "Silent men have the best tales to tell."

Moon felt a little giddy. Unlike Nick, he had no notion of how to amuse a lady.

"I know a game," she said. "It's called—"

"I ain't much of a one for games."

"Well, you should be, Mr. Moon. You are far too serious."

A dreamer, Mae had called him. Moonstruck. Moon's heart twisted inside his chest. His beautiful girl. "Somebody told me different one time."

"Well, they're wrong," she said. "Anyway. Do you want to play my game?"

"I ain't sure," Moon said.

"It's called 'Truth.' I ask a question, and you have to answer truthfully. No deception allowed. And if you do, then you get to ask me a question."

Moon said nothing.

"Oh, Mr. Moon," she said, "don't be glum."

Moon straightened up and tried to assume some appropriate expression.

"Are you ready?"

"I guess."

Claire thought for a moment. "I know," she said. "What's the worst thing you've ever done?"

"Sassed my mama," Moon said.

"No, really, Jim. You have to say true."

Moon hesitated.

"You don't care for me even just a tiny bit, then?" she said.

"Course I do."

She turned away.

"It's just . . ." Moon wasn't always comfortable with the truth.

"I don't have your confidence," she said.

"No. I mean, yes. You do."

She turned around and faced him, steadied him with her eyes. "Then tell me," she said.

Moon took a breath. He scrambled for something to say and found himself talking about the war. He told her about a young soldier he killed. "Surprised him, back in the woods, playing off. He didn't deserve to get shot."

"No one does."

"I know, but . . ."

Claire walked on. "I have a feeling that's not the worst," she said.

Moon was a poor marksman. Cobb was pretty good. "Shoot anyhow," Cobb said.

But Moon laid down his rifle. "Not no more."

They stood in a line of forty men, looking out over a field. A scruffy ridge rose a hundred yards to the south, and beyond it they could hear horses advancing.

"Something's give out in me," Moon said.

Cobb spit on the ground. "Is that a fact?"

Up and down the line, the boys leaned into the stone breastworks, their dark blue caps lined up like beads on a string.

The captain rode up and down behind them. "Hold your fire," he said. "Let them get in close."

The men heard the horses break into a canter and spread out, the tops of their heads just visible on the ridge. Sounded like a hundred or more. Then they heard the shriek of the sabers drawn and the first piercing yell.

"Ain't none of us like it, Jim," Cobb said.

Moon hunkered down behind the wall. "I'll load for you."

Horses appeared on the ridge, gray riders. They topped it and started down, picking their way through the brush. There was a creek at the bottom, rocky and difficult to negotiate, but they'd come on hard once they got across it, the ground opening up flat and grassy.

"Stand up, you goddamned coward." Cobb gave Moon a kick and leaned into the breastwork, taking aim. A yell went up. The first man was across. Moon peeked over the wall and saw him dig into his horse's flank with the heel of his boot and lean forward.

"Hold, hold!"

Ten men were across, fifteen. Moon's heart seemed to stop. He felt he was hardly breathing. Twenty men were over the creek and starting across the field, thirty, forty. Behind them a wall of Confederate infantry rose at the top of the ridge and started scrambling down, a flood of gray.

"Now!"

Cobb fired, handed his rifle down and took Moon's. He fired again. "Hurry!"

Cobb had his own rifle again, fired it and handed off. Moon was slow. The reb cavalry was closing in at a dead gallop. Cobb reached down again before Moon was ready. Their hands fumbled together and triggered the rifle.

The side of Moon's face opened like a flower, and blood splattered Cobb's trousers, a lacy constellation of tiny red stars.

Claire was shaken. "My eye was gone," Moon told her. "The right," he said, as though she couldn't see that for herself.

"I shouldn't have asked."

"I sure showed the white feather that time."

"Maybe you were just . . ."

"What?"

"I don't know. Wise."

They walked on, toward the *Republic*, the statue of a majestic golden woman looking west. "Look at her shine," Moon said.

Claire stopped and turned toward him. She put her hand on his arm. "I'm sorry," she said. "I'm too forward sometimes. I shouldn't have pried."

But, having begun to think back over things, Moon couldn't stop. He found himself telling about Colonel Deal and the rebel boy, so like an angel, his faithful comrades, the little green graveyard, the white gazebo.

"The boy was just being foolish," she said.

"I guess."

The green and the white and the boy, so true to his cause, the way he ran, laughing, innocent. "I killed myself," Moon told her.

"Oh, no. Mr. Moon."

"My own self," he said.

"Delmar Avery's going to France," Caroline told Winslow one evening at supper. "Volunteered to fight for the cause."

"When was that?" Win said.

"Well, he hasn't actually—"

"I read some Harvard boys were over in France on holiday and joined the French army right the minute the war broke out," Mother Maythorpe said. "Imagine. The whole world is at war."

Caroline took a pork chop and passed the platter to Win. "Delmar's having a uniform made at Gilmore's in Winterset," she said. "He has a sidearm and everything."

"You mean a *pistol?*" Mother Maythorpe said.

Caroline helped herself to peas and carrots. "Seems like Delmar Avery's always right in the middle of things."

Win chewed savagely on a crust of bread. Avery had long been his rival—bigger, tougher, handier with his fists. He once pounded Win to a paste over possession of a cigarette card and was fond of pranks: gluing Win's lunch pail shut, tying his laces together. The first boy in the eighth grade to smoke, Delmar was also a master practitioner of the hot foot. It was no surprise, therefore, that he had once again done the manly thing—or at least was thinking about it—way before Win even realized that it was there to be done.

Caroline speared a good-sized baked potato. "My, but I do so admire a soldier."

Win left the house right after supper, headed for Eule Seymour's field. Lately he had begun to spend a considerable part of his afternoons in the bell tower of the Open Bible Church, climbing the circular staircase—on tiptoe so that Pastor wouldn't hear—and wedging himself in among the cobwebs and coiled bell rope in a corner of the cramped wooden cupola. From that height he could see the gravestone hidden out in the cornfield.

Nestled under the iron bell, Win would pray furiously for guidance, his eyes clamped shut and his hands squeezed tightly together. But whenever he got to the part, "Forgive us our debts," one eye would invariably pop open, and there was the stone, lying between the furrows, solid as sin with the flat face of the Book of Life open toward him.

Now in the twilight, he cut across Mother Maythorpe's yard and picked up the road running west a few doors down. Darkness was settling in along the horizon. Lights were coming on in the houses he passed, the windows like thick squares of ancient amber.

Delmar Avery's going to France. Delmar Avery's going to France. You'd think nobody had ever gone there before.

The dust had settled along the road, and the air was cool. Win passed Varner's store and the church, dark and locked up for the night, the cemetery with its listing Civil War stones and ancient pines, its high iron gate. When he reached Seymour's field, he ducked through the sagging barbed-wire fence.

Win had left the stone lying crosswise in a furrow. Now he hoisted it upright and rocked it into position. He leaned against it. Out in the country, away from all the confusion at Sweetbriar, the stone seemed to take on a dignity. It seemed to be true. Win straightened his shoulders and felt the town at his back: Pastor in his study, Caroline and Mother Maythorpe finishing up in the kitchen—drying dishes, pouring out the last of the coffee, putting the soiled table linens to soak. Children were roaming through happy dreams. Men sat under the lamplight, reading the war news in the paper, and only Win was there, out on the land.

A sanctuary rose up around him, growing like prairie grass, imagined walls. A rapt, invisible flock shuffled into their pews, the rustle of their clothing like cornhusks tossed by the wind.

They looked up at Winslow. Their pastor. And Win raised his arms in benediction. "Dearly beloved." No, too formal. "Brothers and sisters in Christ."

He bowed his head and rambled through the Lord's Prayer, the Twenty-third Psalm. He said grace, several versions, then fell silent, stumped for a theme, and waited for inspiration. Preaching would not be easy. Seemed like all the good ideas were taken. Furthermore, a man of God had to be on the straight and narrow himself. Maybe he should wait for a definite calling.

Win looked out on the fields, which rolled away into pure distance, layer on dim layer in shades of blue. Like time, Win thought, like history. He imagined again Moon's heroic moment, how that malevolent ball had selected the bravest man on the field, how Moon, hit over and over again—from the left, the right—had lifted his hands to his face, and beautiful ruby red blood had seeped through his fingers.

Sometimes Moon fell. Sometimes he only wavered a little, staggered and found his balance again, assisted, or sometimes not, by a faithful companion—maybe a colored boy, Win imagined. Always, however, Moon shook off any attempt to lead him from the field, tied the makeshift bandanna and kept on fighting.

Fathers. How their deeds come down to us, he thought, their stories. Shape us. Win felt ennobled by his father's courage, and he knew he was not alone. Many must have been changed by Moon's example.

Win felt a thesis stirring. How kinship moves not only forward through time, the generations, but outward from the center of a life well lived, like ripples on a pond.

Fathers, fatherhood. Win took out his diary and made some notes. Pastor had said the pulpit was his, any time he was ready. He cleared his throat. He needed to practice. Pitching his voice low, like Pastor's, well within the somber range of wisdom, he said the Pledge of Allegiance and recited the Gettysburg Address. He started in on the Declaration of Independence, got as far as "Life, Liberty and the pursuit of Happiness" and stopped. A subtle wind was easing down the corn rows, like a voice whispering in the dark.

"Father?"

A barn owl swept over the corn, hunting. Win had read that they found their prey by listening, sound alone. They didn't need their big, blank eyes.

He closed his own eyes and tried to take in the darkness, the scurry of a possum off in the corn, the sigh of the wind. The lush air of the summer night was so thick and fragrant it seemed that he could gather it in his hands.

"Our Father." Win knelt beside the stone and prayed automatically. "Who art in heaven." Almost immediately he began to falter.

My, but I do so admire a soldier.

He started over. A Father in heaven. Win tried to picture Him, a majestic, white-bearded source of order, but where the heavenly throne should have been, buzzing with cherubs and translucent with light, he saw instead a night sky alive with fire.

How was it possible? Poor little Belgium was fighting bravely, but Caroline said it was only a matter of time. The German plan was to sweep north, outflanking the French border fortifications, and take Paris before Russia could mobilize its troops on the eastern front. The Schlieffen Plan, it was called, an intricate mass movement of men and equipment, horses, guns.

"Thy kingdom come . . ."

Sheet lightning fanned up on the horizon. A wind tossed the switch grass along the fence and made a sound like the stir of wings. Win counted: one, Mississippi; two, Mississippi. Thunder rolled in the north.

The storm was near, then. Half a mile away. How close was thunder to cannonfire? The papers said the ground shook when the big guns fired. Men went mad with the noise of the shelling.

He ran his hands over the stone, and it set up a tingling. Another splash of blue-white lightning struck, low, closer, blanching the ground. The trees along the horizon, birch and big dark cottonwoods, were sharply etched. They moved in the wind like a line of advancing soldiers.

"Father."

How could it have happened? The King of England and the King of Germany were cousins, Win had read in the Winterset paper, both descendants of Queen Victoria. Alliances and treaties and all this and that, and yet the world was spinning out of control.

"Is there going to be any money?" the girl said. "I mean like a reward or something. When this is all settled up?"

The policeman hesitated, his hand on the door. "Sure. Bound to be," he said. "Something."

The girl slid off the bed and dropped to her knees. She pulled a heavy, battered footlocker from underneath the bed. "Well, then."

She sat back on her heels while the policeman knelt and rifled through the contents. "A Civil War jacket," he said, "what's left of it. A photograph of the old coot, and more drawings. That all you got to show me?"

He stood up and dusted his hands.

"Don't go," she said.

He kicked the footlocker shut.

"He was a spy." The girl glanced up, checking his expression. "Worser stuff than that."

"That old codger there. Sure, I believe you." The policeman picked up the photo of Moon, taken late in his life. Light fell on the high forehead, bleaching the skull and shadowing deep hollows at the temples and under the broad, high cheekbones. His hair was long. A gray ballooning beard covered the lower half of his face. The one good eye was perfectly round, haunted, pleading, lonely, gentle, wry.

"Look at this." The girl held up a regimental patch from a uniform. "Confederate," she said. She smoothed the patch with her thin fingers. "And him a Union soldier. Where'd that come from? And these books?" She held up two worn volumes. "Read them for yourself if you want proof."

"What good is a book?"

"You'd be surprised."

She opened a green clothbound book but hardly looked at the pages, and in a reedy, sing-song voice she recited:

> Urge and urge and urge,
> Always the procreant urge of the world.
>
> Out of the dimness opposite equals advance, always
> substance and increase, always sex . . .

"Let me see that."

She closed the book and held it up so he could read the cover.

"*Leaves of Grass*," he said, bewildered. "Grass don't have no leaves."

Rain fell on the White City. Inside the iron skeletons, the men built fires to illuminate the darkness. Jim Moon, using a blacksmith's hammer, was shaping a horseshoe nail around a length of lead pipe to form a ring.

"Bee-you-ti-ful," the little man said. "Claire's gonna love that."

Moon said nothing.

"Matter of fact, though, the lady has other plans."

"Oh? And how'd you know that?"

"I, sir, am Claire voyant. See all, know all."

"And never shut up."

Moon slipped the nail off the pipe and polished it on his pants leg. "This ain't for her anyhow."

The little man scoffed. "I hope you ain't thinking to buy your way back home with that little trinket. Mae Moon would throw you out on your ear."

Moon whirled around. "What do you know about her?"

"Not a thing."

"Don't be flapping your gums, then."

Moon scowled and turned away. "I don't know why I even talk to you."

"Moonie, in fact, you do," the little man said. "I'm the key to what you're after, which is beauty, and truth. Actually, beauty or truth, take your pick."

"I ain't listening."

"'Beauty is truth, truth beauty.' Ever hear that one?"

"I don't know," Moon said.

"Believe that, Moon, my boy, and you are a goner."

"I don't believe in anything," Moon said.

"A patent lie."

Moon slipped the ring in his pocket.

"I might add in my defense," Nick said, "that I am famous for my company. Bon vivant, roué, and raconteur." He executed a neat turn, held his skinny arms out like a showman. "I'm irresistible, to men and to women. Claire herself is deeply in love with me."

"That's a lie," Moon said.

"Of course it is."

"I'm taking her to supper," Moon said. "Soon as I get some money."

"Oh, I see. Money." The little man studied Moon. "And what about Mae?"

Moon wouldn't answer.

"Can't have everything. Or everybody."

"I don't want—"

"Moon, you don't know *what* the hell you want. You never did."

Moon walked away and the little man followed. "Course, you know, a real man'd have a ruby. Least a pearl. Little chip diamond," he said. "Ain't you a real man?"

"Why don't you leave old Moon alone?" a voice called out of the darkness.

Nick turned. His eyes swept the darkness beyond the fire where the other homeless men were huddled together. Abruptly there was a hollow silence. "That's more like it," he said.

"How's a man know he's a man anyways?" Nick went on. "I'll tell you that one. Action."

Rain beat down steadily, reminding Moon of dried grain, the rustle of corn when he shelled it, the kernels falling into a bushel basket, Iowa and the farm. On rainy days, Mae made potato soup and dark rye bread. And pie—apple, peach. Whatever was bearing.

"Remember that Johnstown flood?" the little man said. "Dam broke. Whole reservoir came down. Terrible. Water rushing through town like a freight train. I was there."

Nobody answered him.

"Long, steady rain like this. Regular frog strangler. I was up in the mountains, of course. Pittsburgh swells and their la-di-da South Fork Fishing and Hunting Club—Mellon and Carnegie, Frick and them—invited me."

Silence.

"I was there to inspect the Cambria ironworks, with an eye to investment." The little man pointed his bamboo cane at the rafters. "Iron."

Jim Moon's eyes followed the cane. Every man's eyes looked up. A network of blackened iron hung over them.

"That's what America is, you know, steel and iron, railroads. And men like Pullman and Cyrus McCormick and them. Real men, big men, who know how to seize an opportunity."

"Yeah, well, iron don't burn." Jim Moon hunkered down by the fire.

"There's more'n one way to keep warm."

Moon ignored him.

"Let's draw us a Frisco circle," the little man said. "Throw your change in, boys, and I'll get us a jug."

Nobody moved.

"You boys a little short these days? Haw, haw, haw."

The rain continued. Water seeped through the staff and ran down the inside walls, pooled at the men's feet. Here and there a bucket was placed to catch the rain for drinking water.

"Two thousand two hundred people dead, drowned. Men, women, and children." Nick drew his threadbare coat around him. "What's that to a big boss, hey?"

"Why don't you shut up for a while?"

"I was there."

"You was everywhere," somebody said. "Hear you tell it, you seen everything. Heaven and hell and judgment day."

The little man smiled.

"Who are you anyways? Where you come from?"

The little man tilted his derby forward, shading his glittering eyes. "Oh, you know me all right."

The girl produced the second book, a richly embossed quarto-sized volume, bound in blood-red morocco. She handed it to the policeman.

"Another book." He paged through it.

"I was saving it back," she said.

"Is that a fact?"

"It's a special book, the devil's book."

"Oh, the devil, is it?"

"That's what I heard."

"And you want me to read it to you. Is that it?"

"I ain't sure."

The girl sat on the bed, watching his eyes.

"You really can't read, can you."

She shook her head.

"You know, if you dance with the devil, you pay the piper. You might learn something here you don't want to know."

Mae lay on the bed. She'd had five gentlemen callers the night before. *Visitors*, the madam called them, most of them businessmen. The first time she had been terrified, struggled, actually struck the man, and when he finally understood that he was the first, he gave her something—a curative, he said—to calm her down.

The second had been a thin young man, as shy and frightened as she was. "I'm giving you the easy ones," the madam had told her that first night. "Don't get used to it."

It was early morning, five or six o'clock. Mae stretched out on the bed, too tired to cry. She had given that up anyway, months ago. Her face and neck burned. Her mouth was dry. Somehow she had cut her hand. A broken glass? She couldn't remember. There were other wounds, too, which she didn't care to examine.

The day here was for sleeping, but back home they would just be waking up, the baby, hungry, maybe still wanting his mother, and Mrs. Ross coaxing him back to sleep like she used to do, savoring those last, luxurious minutes in bed. Mae saw his round, blue eyes wide open, his chubby hands reaching out for her. Little Winnie. The mourning doves would soon begin to murmur in the lilac outside the window, and maybe a breeze would stir the curtains. The day would come on hazy, pale, a peach glow spreading along the horizon.

· · ·

The red morocco was ornamented with intricate tooling, some of it stained in gilt. It wrapped the book like a spider's web. "Pretty, ain't it?" she said.

"Yeah, so?"

"See anything?"

"Where?"

"Turn it upside down," she said.

The policeman's face showed nothing at first, then puzzlement, then shock.

"See 'em?" she said.

"Yeah."

Within the intricate arabesque of the ledger's morocco cover, tiny figures squirmed in indecent postures, human and animal swirled, and there wasn't one that wasn't connected by hand or mouth or worse to another, and some of them were doing things the policeman had never imagined doing before.

The girl leaned back on her elbows. "Read to me."

THE MOROCCO BOOK:

Chicago, Illinois, U.S. of A. Fastest growing place on earth—and the wickedest. I was there. Get-it City. Any man with a scheme, any girl with an itch—rich! Overnight, never mind how. And using the rubes for fodder. There was a man, for instance, had a house at Wallace and Sixty-third, H. H. Holmes by name, who liked to "experiment." So a few girls end up with the white slavers, a few country boys get rolled in the Bad Lands by me and my partner, Mickey Finn. Hell, there's more where they came from. They're flooding in.

The little man drew a big circle in the dirt and sat down inside it, pulled a pint of rye from his coat pocket. "Moonie, my boy, let's go traveling."

"I'll have some of that," a voice in the darkness said.

"Aye."

"Oh, no, you don't," the little man said. "This here's just for me and my good friend, Moon."

Grumbling from the shadows. The little man waved his cane. "You boys take a rest now," he said. The men complained for a while, then settled down, and pretty soon Moon heard the snort and whistle of men asleep and snoring loudly in the dark.

"I'm a little particular who I drink with," Moon said.

It was almost midnight. The rain was still falling steadily. Nick had his red morocco book, a bottle of jet black ink beside him, a crow-quill pen tucked behind his ear. "Come on, Moon," he said, "it's just you and me. Your fairyland's melting. You're cold and hungry, poor. You ain't found it, whatever it is you're after. Your girlfriend's way too smart for you. Your baby boy wouldn't know his dear old pap from a load of hay. Your little wife's forgot all about you, and what's the kicker is, you don't even love her."

"I do too," Moon said.

"Sure you do. That's why you're here."

The little man waved the liquor under Moon's nose. "If ever I seen a feller who needed a drink."

Moon reached for the bottle.

"Ah, ah, ah," the little man said.

"What?"

"Come into my parlor, said the spider to the fly." Nick patted the dirt beside him, and Moon moved in close.

THE MOROCCO BOOK:

Best brothel in Chi Town was Carrie Watson's place. Most depraved belonged to Mary Hastings. Lots of corn-fed innocents, fresh off the farm. Vina Fields kept seventy girls working, sometimes eighty. And I mean working.

· · ·

Moon settled down inside the circle, and Nick passed him the bottle. They drank, taking turns, saying nothing. The rain beat relentlessly on the staff of the crumbling building.

"You all wore out," the little man said.

"I'm all right."

"Sure you are. Rest yourself there, pilgrim. You seen a lot."

Moon relaxed. Nick's raspy voice sang on in his ear. "Yes, sir, the White City. The city of your dreams! Everything here a man could imagine, *more*. 'Member you told me about that grassy grave you come from, Mae Greentree's place? All cobbled together." Nick took a drink. "How's a man like you even know *how* to want what you want, that's what I'd like to know."

"I want . . ."

"Daddy's picture on the wall, Mother stuffed into her whalebone corset, harnessed together and working like a pair of goddamned mules."

Moon smiled.

"That's what she wanted for you."

"I love her."

"Sure you do. But, Moon, is that enough?"

Moon took a drink.

"Is anything, ever?" The little man took a drink. "Moon, you are aptly named."

Changeable, he was—the man was right. Romantic, foolish, a reflected light, a seeker, cold, embodying such yearning, such disdain.

"I can just imagine you in your travels," Nick said. "Round them campfires, in your dreams. Changing. You and that—what was his name?"

"Cobb."

"Your little failure of nerve." Nick chuckled and took a drink. "Leaving the wife, the home place, looking forward, looking back. And then, on the steamer that first day. I knew who you was the minute I seen you."

Moon was getting sleepy. "Who?" he said.

"Why, boy, you the forever traveler." Nick slapped his knee and laughed. "Want. I knew you. Big old saucer eye. Thought you had it there for a while. Heaven on earth." Nick took a drink. "You got a long ways to go."

Moon said nothing.

"And now they snatching it right out from under your nose."

Moon sat up.

"You know what your problem is, Ioway?" Nick said. "Contrast. Take a drink."

Moon waved him off. He felt dizzy. He tried to stand.

"Sit down, Moon, and keep them eyes—correction, that *eye*—closed."

"I'm getting drunk," Moon said.

"Worse things could happen."

The little man put his arm around Moon's shoulder. "Climb the stairs with me, Moon."

Moon, drifting into sleep, shifted his weight against the little man.

"Open the door," the little man said, "and walk right in. Carrie Watson's parrot says, *Evenin', gents.*

"Bunch of silk hats sitting around the parlor, talking bidness—regular tower of Babel. Parlez-vous, parvenus? Betcha do. Gents, my good friend, Moon."

Moon, dreaming, nods, smiles, embarrassed, wipes his hands on his pants, and feels the horseshoe nail ring in his pocket.

"Ain't no better than us, Moon. Not a bit."

The little man struts on the carpet, hat tipped back, addressing the gentlemen. "Don't be high and mighty, boys. Year ago you was boomers like me and Moon, taking them midnight zippers, bumming nickels. Look at you now. Whoa."

Silence. Just the swing of golden watch chains, just the smoke from big cigars. Eyes as blank as silver dollars. Business.

"How's about we talk Eye-talian?" Nick says. "You no speak?

Greek? German? Bunch of Jews." He spits. "Not our sort, Moonie, not a bit."

Silence.

"I detect hostility here. Class divisions, ethnic differences. Moon and me is sure in the wrong pew. Phew! Open the door, Jim Moon, we're traveling on."

THE MOROCCO BOOK:

Me and Moon stumble out, night as black as the ace of spades and not a star in the sky. No moon in Custom House Place. Still, the Moon is out, if you get my drift.

"Where we at?" This from my man, Moon.

"Allow me to orientate you. Look around."

Moon looks.

"What do you see?"

"Nothing."

"There you go."

Trolley cars moving like dung beetles, black as your hat, narrow streets and skyscrapers blocking the moon. Empty wallets and horse manure, human turds, false teeth, blood, hair—not its natural color—and there's more: bewilderment and lost love, aspiration and undelivered letters, guilt that nothing can fix, and failure, hope, and, of course, that old everlasting want floating down the gutters.

"What's white?"

I'm asking Moon. He looks at me, moon-faced, and I tell him, "Moon, why, everything." I have to answer for Mr. Moon, who is speechless.

"What's black? The absence of white."

"But . . ."

"How do you know what's what, what's white, what's right? Why, simple: Sample. Moonie, my boy, may I present the black city."

.   .   .

Moon woke, leaned out of the circle. The little man pulled him back. "Mr. Moon, you are very drunk. I shall take you to Mike Mc-Donald's store to sober you up and try your luck. No, by George, I'll take you to Mary Hastings's. There's a woman there now I think you know. Come from Ioway, fresh off the farm. Open the door, Jim Moon, and walk right through."

Moon stood up, weaving. He fell. He dreamed.

The stairs tilt, in motion. They go up, endless, to nowhere. They go down and down and down. Windows float, through which Moon sees the face of every man and woman he's loved.

"Coming through!" A green-eyed harlot, marked by smallpox, dressed in red, rubies at her throat like drops of blood. She passes close. "Mr. Moon," she says.

A prairie opens out in ivory and gold and sage-green grasses, stretching as far as the eye can see. A sky that is limitless. A herd of fat buffalo, a flock of soft gray passenger pigeons.

Another whore backs down the stairs. She lifts her skirt and shows her dimpled buttocks. They all know him. Washington Roebling, suffering from caisson disease, wheels his chair past Moon — the man, Moon remembers, who built the Brooklyn Bridge from his father's design.

"A force at rest is at rest because it is balanced by some other force," Roebling remarks, "or by its own reaction."

Moon marvels. In other words, a fine network of tensions, a movement in stasis, caught, suspended, suspension bridge, a war at peace.

Roebling spins away. "A force at rest . . ." Moon catches sight of the bridge in the distance. The Eighth Wonder. Poets sing it. Brooklyn Bridge. At last. Moon's rendezvous.

THE MOROCCO BOOK:

The best of them was Mabel Clay, a big woman with pale flesh and hair the color of anthracite, who came from Kansas City and all points west. She had nails a dark maroony red that men who knew her said she flexed like cat's claws. Cat's eyes. Triple-lidded and greenback green.

At Mary Hastings's the stairs led to a hallway that narrowed, swayed like a rope bridge. Moon, suspended, pursuing unadulterated whiteness, stepped on. He met a man, all wet, who looked quite Moony: *And what I assume you shall assume.* The sound of an engine, strange animal noises from various quarters, water lapping against the side of a boat.

"They's doors on every side," Nick said. He tapped them with his cane, and they swung wide open. "Take a look-see, Moon, and learn you something."

A woman was washing her hair in silver dimes. A woman was licking the diamond ring on the hand of a fat businessman. Down on her knees, working. Crude oil in a bathtub. Coal dust drifting across the floor. Influenza and typhoid. Money, money, money. Malaria. The sound of trains and relentless pounding, children crying, coins rolling down the hall like a rushing wind, tilting, spilling, coins of all nations—francs, marks, lire, rubles, shillings. They cut a hollow spiral right through the heart of emptiness, a river, a tide, an avalanche.

Moon couldn't keep his footing, fell, was dragged into a room by invisible (wet and bony) hands. *Every atom belonging to me . . .* A map of cracks on the ceiling, a Persian rug. A gas lamp swinging overhead, brass, the boot of Mabel Clay. She towered above him, and all that Moon saw clearly was her plump black leather ankle and her curd-white calf, tattooed with the bluebird of happiness. "Money, money, money," and Moon offered her all he had: a book, a set of drawings, a horseshoe nail ring. But the wings were spread— the bird was on the wing—and Mabel Clay her own sweet self was spreading out, a satin spread, a blood-red spread. It was want. It was Moon over Mabel Clay over Moon.

Moon and Mabel, rolling. Moon came up for air. Someone in

the shadows, honey-haired, a drunkard's dream, a sad hallucination, seemed to watch them for a while, then vanished. The swirl of her blue skirt, turning, fluttered. Oh . . .

> The bird of time has but a little way
> To flutter—and the bird is on the wing.

Moon was pinned beneath the Clay—"What the hell?"—he struggled, wiggled—"Haw, haw, haw." But Mae was gone, and Mabel, now a woman scorned, was mad as hell and doubled up her fist. She reared back, grinned, and delivered a Haymarket haymaker right between the eyes. Moon sank like a stone and failed to rise.

Part Three

MOON AT THE TOP of a ladder. Noonday sun beating down. Little bitty breeze from off the lake, lifting his thinning hair.

The stir of memory.

Whispering.

Moon in a fever, working, shoring up the city, yet he saw: bodies dripping from off the trees, just on the edge of perception. Hundred and thirty-five colored men lynched that year. Only Moon and a few other people could see them. Only a few could hear the feet of Coxey's Army slowly moving east.

"Moon! Come down!" the little man hollered, but Moon just kept right on.

"What's he doing?" someone said. "What's he up to, Moon?"

"Why's he up there?"

"Working."

"What's he want?"

One hundred thousand mine workers, Washington state to Pennsylvania, out on strike and shutting the country down. Moon took a drink from a bottle he kept in his back pocket and took another step up the narrow ladder.

There was trouble at Pullman, too, hard times and wage disputes. A grievance committee was formed, and on May 7 forty-six Pullman workers met with Thomas Wickes, the company's second vice-president, in his small, cluttered office. Moon tagged along with Billy Barnes, a friend of the committee chairman, Thomas Heathcoate, who explained the urgency of restoring wages to their former levels. The men were worried about their families, Tom told Wickes. "Some of them can barely put bread on the table."

Wickes was a company man, fair but suspicious of labor. Everyone knew there were anarchists among them, fanatics who would pull the system down to achieve their "freedom." He noted Moon in the back of the room, an unfamiliar face.

"Let's go round and introduce ourselves," he said. When it got to Moon, Wickes made a note of the name. "Moon, is it?"

Moon nodded.

"Unusual name."

It was a tactic, of course, calculated not only to collect names but to diminish the men in their own eyes. Who were they, after all, to challenge George Pullman?

"Now that we know each other," Wickes said, folding his arms and leaning back on the desk, "what can I do for you?"

Heathcoate began to speak; then Barnes chimed in. "Wages—"
"By the time the rents are taken out—"

"Boys, boys, one at a time," Wickes said.

The men began to tell their stories. The room buzzed with voices, all except Moon's.

"What's the matter with you, granddad?" somebody asked him. "You're awful quiet today. You happy having your wages cut?"

"Maybe he ain't *had* 'em cut. Maybe he's got friends."

Moon protested. "I'm—"

"You're mighty suspicious is what you are."

The men turned their backs on Moon and began to speculate. "Probably a spy," somebody said. "Odd-looking cuss." "They say there's one or two in every department."

Meanwhile Wickes was studying Moon's features, memorizing the wild, frizzy hair, the angular frame, the eye patch. Not a Pullman worker. Not a union man. Moon, Moon. Who the hell was this old coot?

"We're willing to work," Tom said, summing up.

"Sure," Barnes said. "Every man here wants to keep his job."

"But we need a fair wage, a living." Tom turned to go. "And it's gotta come quick."

That afternoon, Wickes called in a detective. "This old man, Moon," he said. "What have we got on him?"

"Nothing much. No known address. The workers think he might be on our payroll."

"Is he?"

"Nope. Hangs out at them exposition buildings in Jackson Park."

"Just a tramp, then."

"I don't know. He's working on the buildings, I guess. Some kind of carpenter."

"Talk to Barnes." Wickes took a cigar from his desk drawer and lit it. "See what he knows."

The detective was hunched over his notebook, making a list of contacts.

"And that girl, his sister," Wickes said. "What's her name. She's one of those whaddaya call 'em, *suffragists*."

The detective looked up and smiled. "Yeah, I get you," he said. "Birds of a feather."

The committee returned two days later with George Howard, vice-president of the American Railway Union. Harvey Middleton, the Pullman manager, was there with Wickes and some department heads. Moon noted their well-tailored suits, their clean white shirts, and hid his dirty hands behind his back.

The men repeated their demands, but the company's position had not changed: There was nothing, they said, to negotiate.

"Nothing," Moon echoed from the back of the room. "Nothing, nothing."

Heads turned.

"Who's that?" Wickes said. "What's that supposed to mean?"

"That's Moon," somebody said. "He's loony. Don't pay him any mind."

Just then George Pullman appeared, a dapper man with the

slick, blunt hands of a Sunday school teacher and skin as smooth and pink as a girl's. The men crowded forward to press their case.

"Now, now." Pullman raised his hands, a signal for quiet. "What seems to be the problem?"

The same arguments were advanced, the same rebuttals. Finally, Pullman, exasperated, offered to let the men take a look at the books. He wanted to show them, he said, how the Pullman Palace Car Company had been taking contracts at a loss in order to keep them working.

"It's all here," he said. He held up a gray-bound ledger. "In black and white." He spread his arms like an impresario. "I have nothing to hide."

The men were suspicious. They clustered near the door and talked it over, Moon's voice babbling outside the circle. In the end, however, they declined. Two sets of books, perhaps, or some clever alterations. Look at the books, the man said. What would that prove?

"It's them foreigners," Nick told Barnes. "Italians, micks, bohunks. It's them immigrants."

"Don't listen to him," Cora said.

They sat in the Barnes parlor. "Crowding you out of your own damn country."

"Don't trust him, Billy," Cora said.

She didn't like Mr. Nickels, though she would never begrudge any man a meal and a place by the fire. He was no Christian, she felt sure. "All you do is stir up trouble," she told him.

"Me?"

"Whispering in his ear."

"Ain't me." The little man helped himself to an oatmeal cookie. "It's them outsiders, missus. Working for less than a decent man ought to take."

"No, it's the bosses," Barnes said.

"Okay, okay." Nick leaned forward. "What are you gonna do about it, then?"

. . .

The sight and smell and texture of wood stirred up possibilities for Moon, soothed him in the contemplation of snug houses and tight barns. The soft fall of curling pine from a plane, the drift of sawdust, the certainty in the hammering of nails kept him steady. Likewise, the acrid smell of paint, the slap of a brush, the feel of his hands on rough rope, hauling.

"A natural-born builder," the little man shouted up to Moon. "Just what the times demand. Sheecargo man, but looka here . . ."

Moon was rebuilding the city, replacing lath, mixing staff and slapping it on. He had completed a swath some twenty feet high along the east side of the Manufactures Building and planned to build some sort of scaffolding so he could lower himself from the roof to finish the job. A pile of lumber was stacked at the foot of the ladder, a keg of nails, a sack of plaster of Paris, and white lead paint, all of which he had scrounged at various building sites downtown. Roaming the Loop at night, drinking, disoriented and talking to himself in a steady buzz of consternation, Moon found tools to borrow: rope and ladders, hooks and augers, a hatchet, an adze, a bucket, a brush.

"Moon, you are a lunatic. You look, but you don't see. This here's yesterday." The little man swept his arm in a wide arc that encompassed the whole of the White City. "It's skyscrapers now, Moonie, brick and steel."

Moon took a pull on the bottle, blinked back the glare all around him and tried to think. Change, change, inventions. Destruction and war machines. Politicians were scheming. Paradise. Big business and mass production. What was a working man supposed to do?

A little plaster, a coat of paint. Wasn't it all down in black and white? The biggest, the latest, the greatest, the land of opportunity, rubes. There was nothing to negotiate. The White City. If he could save it, future generations would bless his memory.

Traffic sounds filtered up from the street. A warm breeze blew in through the hotel window.

"You know, if he was up to something," the policeman said, "something illegal . . ."

The girl wasn't listening.

"Guilt by association."

She remembered Moon at the same window, brooding, back when he first took her in. Midnight, one o'clock. A feather bed with clean white muslin sheets and moonlight spilling across the floor, so bright it woke her, moving across the coverlet like a hand and nudging her shoulder.

She sat up and threw back the bedclothes, pulled on her yellow silk wrapper.

"Don't get up," Moon told her.

But she did. Barefoot, she went to him and brushed the hair from his brow. "What's the matter, Moon?" She checked his expression and found the same old restless energy. "Ain't sleepy?"

Moon shook his head.

She stood on tiptoe to kiss the bridge of his nose. The empty eye looked down at her, a cynical pucker.

"You never told me how you done that," she said.

"Big old blackbird come along." Moon made a claw of his fingers and plucked at the sleeve of her wrapper. "Pulled her right out."

The girl smiled. "You're always fooling me."

She leaned against his shoulder and looked out over the city: the hunched shapes of the tenements and, beyond them, the jagged skyline. Across the way a light appeared in a window, and sharp, angry voices started up—accusations, recriminations, oddly muted by night.

"Somebody fighting," the girl said. Moon nodded.

They listened, trying to catch the gist of the argument. "Money," Moon said.

"You think?"

"It's always money now."

The voices rose in a passionate recitative. Shadows appeared on the blind. One towered above the other, advancing. A man and a woman. They danced out of sight, then back again, and the voices rushed to a climax and crashed, crockery breaking, a mirror perhaps.

The light winked out.

"Where do you get your money?"

"What do you care?"

"Don't be mad, Moon."

"Don't be asking me questions."

Moon left the window and crossed the room, took his long brown coat from the hook and draped it over his shoulders like a cape. At the threshold, he turned and told her to lock the door behind him.

"Moon, don't go out," she said.

"I'll be back."

"Please. Let's not go through all that craziness again."

"Go to bed."

"Let me go with you."

"No." Moon was like a stern father sometimes. "Get in bed and go to sleep."

He softened a little then. "I'll be right back." He pulled away and melted into the darkness of the hall.

Moon knew his way, down the hollow stairs. *Money, money.* Only the light from the high windows illuminated the landings. Through the door, across the lobby. Out on the street the air was heavy with summer, breathing, charged as though a spark could set it off.

Moon headed south. The night people, busy getting and spending, leaned from the doorways—*Who goes there?* Moon hailed them. He knew their ways, the flourishing basement economy of flesh and cash and promises, with liquor and cocaine to grease the skids.

Money, money. Moon wanted a drink. Behind a warehouse, down a dark, closed staircase with a quick turn at the bottom, and Moon was in an underground alcove the size of a small parlor. Nothing there but a newspaper pallet, a candle, an empty crate that served as an office desk, and Patch Sullivan, the crooked mick, dispensing booze.

"Credit," Moon said.

"Ah, and good evening to *you*, then," Sullivan said.

"And hurry up."

"On the cuff again, is it?"

Moon shivered and shifted his weight. "I'll pay you. I always do."

Patch grinned, rolled up his shirtsleeves. "You're a goner, Moonie."

"So they tell me."

Sullivan filled a small, flat bottle from a large amber jug, using a funnel and hose to siphon it out. "You know, don't you, Moon, this pop-skull here'll blind your other eye out. That is, if it doesn't kill you first."

Moon was starting to pace. "You just let me worry on that," he said.

"Sure." Patch sealed the bottle and handed it over. "I got troubles of my own," he said.

Back in the room, Mary had fallen asleep. Her face was pale, serene, reflecting no dreams. Moon cut open the bottle, sat down at the table, and took a drink. It was raw, watered rye, but it did the trick, burning away the confusion. Moon closed his one good eye and savored the woody aftertaste. Peace. Solitude. The old comfort that made him feel a little more familiar to himself. Moon was tired. His hand on the table was gnarled as an ancient burr oak and heavy-veined. His legs were oddly angled, like dropped timber.

Money. Money—the only language left. How would the girl make it when he was gone?

Moon walked to the window and stared out. Nothing. An empty street, the refuse of day heaped in the gutters, broken glass and pools of filthy water. Moon remembered stars. So many. Scattered across the sky. So many that, in all his years of rambling, he had never once felt alone. It was not a bad thing to be small and inconsequential out on the land. He had always felt he was caught up in something bigger. August was the brightest month, and Vega, in the Lyre of Orpheus, was the brightest star. Lost Eurydice. Moon took a drink and looked up. The circuit was almost run, for there came Capricorn, advancing out of the south, Aquarius, an old man, hunched under his burden, a water sign.

The storm had passed, leaving only a few damaged gardens, a scatter of leaves brought down by the wind. Winslow climbed the bell tower and, using a spyglass, looked out west to Eule Seymour's field. The stone was still there, tilted a little but upright among the furrows. The pages of the book caught the morning light. Win noticed how the ivy seemed to anchor the stone now, how the calla lilies appeared to blossom among the corn. Some sort of organic fusion had taken place, as though the stone belonged to the land, as though it had always been there.

He sat down and opened his sketchpad, dated the upper right-hand corner—August 22, 1914—and drew a sharp, heavy vertical line. He took a bold approach. In his rendering the stone erupted out of the field. The open book was huge, wildly out of proportion. Etched upon the limestone pages were fragments of ornate script, a passage.

Win stopped to consider. Should he make the words clear, suggest a text? His father must have designed the stone for some reason. What was the truth that the Book of Life had to tell?

He flipped to a new page and started another drawing: a tall, lean man with curly dark hair, seen obliquely, walking away, just the hint of his profile showing, an eye patch, a thin, ambiguous smile. Sunlight washed across the page. Win sketched in a road, running diagonally and dropping off into nothing at the horizon, a setting sun, a shred of cloud. He was so engrossed he didn't hear the pastor's Model T pull up in front of the church door down below.

"Winslow?"

Win looked up. Out past the harness shop, beyond Varner's store, a frame of Canada geese, flying low over Eddy's pond, suddenly shattered, and one, the clown of the flock, flipped in a barrel roll and landed feet first on the water, its webbed toes outstretched in comic grace. Win laughed out loud and turned to a fresh sheet of paper. Not the way starlings fall from a telegraph wire or fat, gray pigeons rustle up—he sketched quickly, a lighter style—no, this was a deliberate confusion, sheer joy, a testing of order.

"Wins-low."

Win's strokes were short and urgent. The goose emerged solid and round, with a wicked glint in his eye. The feet were exaggerated, pushing into the foreground.

"Winslow!"

Damn! Win slammed the book shut and stashed it under a coil of rope. Just when he was getting it. He scrambled down the twisting stairs. "I'm coming," he said.

The responsibility of management was to keep profits high for the investors, Pullman had told his workers. This meant periodic adjustments in wages. But cost-effective management meant steady work, and steady work was a living, and so, in the last analysis, Pullman had said, the goals of labor and management were the same. As for rents, like any other landlord, the Pullman Palace Car Company took no interest in the wages of its tenants. The company as employer and the company as landlord were separate entities, and, after all, no attempt had been made to evict anyone. Pullman had concluded the meeting by telling the workers that they were all his children.

"Children," Billy Barnes said.

"Don't give in to your anger."

"We are all his *children*, that's what he said."

Cora Barnes was a patient woman, a Christian, unlike her husband, who had no abiding beliefs. Billy Barnes was energy, muscle and bone, fuel for American industry. And here was the soft spot: he loved his family.

In a personal way. Unlike Moon, who was abstract, an idealist, a man of vision, Barnes loved the sight and sound and smell of them, the baby with his stiff red hair, the sour smell of him, his toothless laugh, his shit-stained diapers, his fat baby fingers wrapped around a spoon, and Cora, always with a rag in her hand, wiping up oatmeal and spilled milk, and the way, when she was busy, scrubbing, strands of silky chestnut hair would mutiny from the twist on the crown of her head and spill down her neck, which was still pale white and still the softest place, just at the collarbone, to get in close and nuzzle her from behind.

Therefore, his strength could be harnessed. Even his will could be shaped, brokered for the purposes of George Pullman's Pullman Palace Car Company.

"God delivered his children from under Pharaoh," Cora reminded him.

Barnes brought his big fist down on the kitchen table. "Where's our Moses, then?"

A knock at the door. The little man had dropped by to call on Claire, but she wasn't at home. "Heard the news, I guess," he said.

Only that morning, three Pullman workers had been turned away at the factory gate, members of the negotiating committee. The workers called it a "Pullman dismissal," the company claiming there was no work when the three committee men had, in fact, been fired.

"They men are calling a meeting," Barnes said. "After supper."

"Don't, Billy," Cora said. "Don't get involved."

"Your good woman is right," Nick said. "Patience. And a sense of decorum, my man. If the boss wasn't naturally better than you, he wouldn't be the boss, now would he?"

Win lollygagged his way through the morning. At noon, he took his lunch pail and his sketchpad and walked out onto the prairie. It was August. The bright yellow rosinweed was in bloom along the narrow path he had cut from the churchyard to the river. Late goldenrod and purple swamp thistle nodded in the sun, the tiny white blossoms of heath aster.

A line of crows flapped overhead, cawing into the wind. Portentous, noisy, bickering shadows—Win longed for a slingshot. But Pastor said they were "God's necessaries." Scavengers.

Win left the path and waded into a stand of giant bluestem—turkeyfoot, some called it, because of its three-pronged spikelets. Instantly he was swallowed up. The grass was over his head, swaying, whispering in the wind, an ancient sea, and on an impulse he spun, twisting, letting his knees go weak and spreading his arms. He fell backward, trusting the grass to catch him.

And the sky opened up above him. The bluestem sighed. Win heard a rush like breaking water, grass yielding, easing him down. Mud. Cradled at the roots he felt the warm, humid breath of the earth, the steady throb of animal life. A startled field mouse brushed his hair. Beetles, black and shiny as licorice whips, traveled through the tangle of stems, each on some solemn mission, each, like Win, folded into the intricacy of being. Above his head a dragonfly circled. Win watched as it spiraled into the sun.

"Read me a little bit more."

"I can't stay."

The girl picked up the morocco book and held it out to the cop. "It's a good story, I bet. Honest."

The policeman shook his head. "No, love. This business is not honest. That's the one thing it's not."

"Listen."

"How old are you, anyway?" he said.

"Old enough to know better."

"I'd say twenty."

"Say whatever you want."

The policeman studied Moon's picture and glanced up at the girl. "You know what I think?" he said.

She was pouting now.

"I think he's your dad."

The girl said nothing.

"Am I right?"

Nothing.

He handed the picture back.

"So, you won't help me," she said.

"It's not that, girl."

"I was right not to trust you."

The glare of pure white staff in full sunlight was absolute. It dominated the eye. Compelling, Moon thought, and beautiful. The weather was warm enough now for Moon to work in his shirtsleeves. He took another step up the ladder and, looking out over the lake, saw a meadow of blue, netted with whitecaps. A blissful emptiness, a new frontier. Near shore he saw the bulk of the Manufactures Building, reflected, inverted, seemingly submerged, a huge white leviathan waiting beneath the surface.

"Moon? Come down. Big doin's at Pullman," the little man hollered.

Moon chipped away some loose staff and slathered on a fresh white plaster of Paris mixture of his own devising. The trouble with the old mixture was in the adhesive, Moon had decided. And in the additives. Horse hair! Harder to get, but better than straw, and not chopped up too fine—that was the trick—so as to permit the permanent bonding of additive and adhesive.

And, of course, the thing about hair . . .

"Moon!"

. . . animal byproduct, waterproof, as opposed to vegetable matter, which is . . .

"Come down off that ladder!"

Moisture. Straw will soak up water quicker than you can say . . .

"Moon!"

Moisture.

"Hey, Moon!"

That's where the trouble starts.

Caroline stood on the top step of the porch. "Win, what in the world? Look at you," she said, scowling. "Muddy from head to foot."

She peered more closely. "Did you go fishing?"

Ordinarily, Win would have hung his head and taken a scolding. Having no real mother, he accepted whatever punishment women inflicted. Win was a bit of a fatalist, but that was changing.

He looked her straight in the eye. "I went for a walk."

"In a mud puddle?"

"Out on the land."

Caroline was not happy. "Pastor came by and said you disappeared on him. Said you left a pile of papers, supposed to be put away, and something else—I forget. What has got into you?"

Win worked the pump handle until an icy stream of water began to splash over the mossy pump stone. He rinsed his hands, bathed his neck, scooped a double handful of water, and buried his face in the cold.

"Where were you?" she said.

Win stuck his head under the running water.

"I'm talking to you."

A gurgle, a froth of silver bubbles.

"What?"

Win shook his head like a wet dog.

The policeman had his hand on the doorknob. "For what it's worth, Mary, I think you're a fine girl."

"And just what *is* that worth?" she said.

"Look."

"Being a fine girl, I mean."

She laid the morocco book on the table and began to turn the pages. "She's in here," she said. "I know it."

He watched her for a moment. So determined. So vulnerable. Her head bowed. The way, in the gauzy light of late afternoon, her body curved. He crossed the room. "Don't cry," he said.

"I ain't."

He pulled a button off his coat and laid it on the table beside her. "A token," he said. "A peace offering." He bent and kissed the nape of her neck. "You remember me, now."

. . .

Caroline was sarcastic at supper. "I thought we'd be having fish to-night. I thought Mr. Winslow Moon might have brought home a catfish."

"I was not fishing," Winslow said. He poured himself a glass of milk from the pitcher. "And what if I was?"

"You just refuse to take ahold and make anything of yourself," Caroline said.

"What is 'anything'?"

"I think Win is a very levelheaded young man," Mother May-thorpe said.

"Thank you." Win unfolded his napkin. "I don't know that lev-elheadedness is quite the fashion nowadays, however."

"Oh, Win," Caroline said. "I just want you to *be* somebody."

Mrs. Maythorpe brought in a platter of fried chicken, Caroline's favorite. Caroline took a wing and a breast, a helping of mashed potatoes, a roll, a spoonful of green beans with bacon. Between bites, she talked nonstop about wonderful Delmar Avery, who, it seemed, was even more heroic than she had initially realized. He still planned to volunteer, for something, as soon as he found out how to go about it. "War is terribly dangerous," Caroline said. She stripped the wing to the bone. "Of course, Delmar Avery doesn't know the meaning of fear."

"There's lots he don't know," Win said.

Caroline stuck out her tongue. "Jealous."

"Caroline!" Mother Maythorpe was scandalized.

"Well, he *is*."

Caroline stabbed at her chicken breast. "Delmar says every German book in the high school ought to be burned in the square at high noon and every German run out of town on a rail."

"Give 'em time," Win said.

Caroline tore into a roll and slathered it with butter. In ten years or so, Win imagined, the way that girl put away groceries, she would likely outweigh him by thirty-five pounds.

"I heard all of this trouble could have been avoided," he said. "I read in the papers—"

"But it wasn't, was it?" Caroline said. "That's the point. You're always saying 'what if, what if,' but Delmar Avery—"

"Oh, stop about him."

They ate in silence for a while, Mother Maythorpe glancing nervously from Win to her daughter. "Children," she said finally. "Let's don't quarrel."

Win pushed his plate away. "I ain't the one."

Caroline went to the sideboard and dished up the custard pudding. "I'd like to see *you* volunteer."

"I don't *want*—"

"I don't guess you do."

She put his dish in front of him and resumed her place opposite him at the table. "You never said where you were all day."

Silence.

"Were you in town on church business?"

Win dug into his pudding.

"You know, Winnie, if you *were* fishing, I'd forgive you."

Win gave her a sour smile.

"Pastor says, he can't keep a young man on who doesn't have a sense of—"

"Pass the cream," Win said.

"So where were you?"

Win looked up, thoughtful, his spoon suspended over his pudding dish. "I was about my father's business," he said.

The little man returned after supper and knocked on the Barneses' front door.

"Why, where's Mr. Moon?" Cora said. "We're used to seeing the two of you as a pair."

"Mr. Moon is irrelevant on this occasion," Nick said. He seated himself in the parlor, his derby hat on his knee. His thick red hair was slicked down, and his long fingernails had been cleaned and neatly pared.

Cora was surprised, confused. "I'll get Alice," she said, disappearing into the kitchen. "I mean, Claire."

Nick studied his surroundings. Typical working-class taste. A maroon horsehair sofa, a little the worse for wear; a walnut mantel clock that struck the hour and half-hour in hollow, wavering tones; an imitation Eastlake library table displaying a well-thumbed, leather-bound Bible; a mourning wreath in a gilt frame; and centered over the iron fireplace, a formal wedding portrait of Ma and Pa Barnes, looking stunned and apprehensive.

"Never a damned spittoon when you need one," he said.

In the kitchen Claire protested. "I don't want to see him," she said, "alone."

"Well, we can't just leave him sitting in there."

"Where's Billy?"

Cora hung her head. "I don't know. Gone to that union meeting, I'm afraid."

"You'd best *be*, missus," the little man said. He stood in the kitchen doorway, holding his derby hat in his hands. "Afraid, I mean."

Nick strolled in and seated himself at the table. "I hear that Pullman detective come around."

"He stopped by," Claire said. "What of it?"

Nick looked at Cora. "You better watch that hotheaded husband of yours."

"I don't think my brother's business is any of yours," Claire said. "And if you don't mind my saying so—"

"Dangerous work."

Claire stopped. "Do you think so?"

"The bosses don't like confusion."

Claire turned to Cora and took her hand. "It's going to be all right. Don't worry."

"I thought we could take a walk," the little man said.

"Not tonight."

"I got some interesting news about old Billy."

The women rushed forward. "Where is he? Is he all right?"

The little man stood up. "I'm not facing no female inquisition."

"Please."

"Take a walk with me, Claire—just you—and maybe I can give you some information."

They left the house and walked south, silent at first. The evening was mild, and women and children were sitting out on the porches.

"What about Billy?" Claire said.

"Who?"

"Stop it," she said. "Cora's wild with worry."

"He's all right." Nick lit a cigar. "Far as I know."

"So you don't really have any information."

"I just said that to get you to come out."

Claire stopped and turned to face him. "Mr. Nickels," she said, "I don't think we should try to maintain our friendship."

"That a fact?"

"I don't believe we even *have* a friendship."

"Do tell."

She stood her ground, glaring. "Mr. Nickels," she said finally, "I know you probably won't answer me . . ."

"Yes?"

"Oh, what's the use in talking to you."

"My dear, if you have a question . . ."

"Why?" she said. "Why? That's my question."

Nick chuckled. "The old *eternal* question."

"You go out of your way to make everything . . . wrong. You confuse every situation."

He took her hand and tucked it under his arm, bowed his head toward her. Anyone passing by might have thought they were husband and wife.

Claire began to struggle. "Let go of me."

"In a minute," he said.

They walked in silence, past the graceful Hotel Florence, its windows aglow with light, past the double-doored stable with its warm, grassy smell.

The little man led Claire down a narrow side street.

"You know, girl," he said, "I haven't been quite honest with you."

"That doesn't surprise me."

"About my feelings, I mean."

He stopped and extinguished his stogie on the sole of his shoe. He put the stub in his pocket. "Now, feelings is tough."

"I suppose they are, for a man like you."

"Tough to express."

Claire tried to pull away, but Nick held on to her arm.

"The truth is, I'm in love with you, girl."

"I beg your pardon."

The little man smiled. "I'm asking for your hand."

The girl had the button folded in her hand. "You don't give a damn about that old man," she said. "You're just after the money."

"I'm doing my job," the policeman said.

"You don't care about me either," she said.

"I care. But you and me . . ."

"Read me the rest of it."

He shook his head. "Sure, this is only a game you're playing," he said. He walked to the door.

"No. Please. I've almost figured it out."

He turned around and gave her a blank look.

"Who she was."

"Look, you're very pretty," he said. "You're very easy to talk to."

"His name is Moon."

The door stood open. A warm breeze filtered in.

"You mean like up in the sky?" the policeman said.

"Moon. Jim Moon. James. James Ransom Moon."

The policeman stepped back inside and closed the door. "Why are you telling me now?"

"Mr. Nickels, you're mad," Claire said. "Marriage indeed."

The little man let go of her hand. "You want to think this over, missy. You don't know what happens to girls alone."

"I'm not alone. I have my family. I have friends."

"Women is all."

"Women are good companions."

"Let me tell you a little story," he said.

"I don't want to hear any stories from you."

"About another woman, came here from Iowa, looking for her husband, who had flown the domestic coop, if you get my drift. Left her to seek his fame and fortune here in the Windy City."

"What are you talking about?"

"This woman—no man around, see, to protect her—got herself mixed up with the white slavers. You've heard of them. And knocked up, to use the polite term." He shook his head sadly. "A common occupational hazard, I am led to believe."

"She became a . . . prostitute?"

"Alas, a soiled dove."

"I don't care to hear any more about it." Claire turned and started to walk away.

The little man grabbed her wrist, pulled her close, and stared into her eyes. "Her employer was sorely disappointed. Them mothers-to-be is bad for bidness. Know what she did?"

Claire was fascinated. She shook her head.

"Well, she suggested the old calisaya, of course, other poisons, knitting needles, all the standard home remedies. Even tried to tumble her down the stairs a time or two, but this working girl, the one I'm telling about, she fought back. Regular wildcat. Wanted to keep the little bastard, a fatherless baby or—let me put this delicately—a baby with an overabundance of fathers. Stubborn as a load of bricks, this girl. Course, the madam threw her out. Wouldn't you? And where do you think she ended up at?"

Claire was afraid of him now.

"Walking the streets. Picking up gentlemen friends and going down on her knees to pray for them in the alleys. Doing them four-bit knee-tremblers."

"I'm going back." Claire tried to shake loose, but the little man held her tight.

"You ain't answered my question."

"No. No, I wouldn't marry you if . . ."

"I was the last man on earth?"

"Yes. No."

"The richest?"

"Let go of me."

"You turn me down, girl, I'll make you sorry you ever met me."

"I'm sorry already, you . . . demon."

For once, the little man was surprised. "Demon?"

"That's exactly what you are."

He let go of her wrist and stepped back, taking her measure, perhaps for the first time. An odd smile played on his lips. "Some day *you'll* lose somebody you love," he said.

"You're not in love with me."

"Love, lust, what's the difference? Anyhow, I'll fix you, sooner or later."

"Go ahead and try. I'm not afraid of you."

"Feisty, hey? I like a gal with spunk."

"I'm not your 'gal.'"

The little man buried his hands in his pockets and studied the walkway. "Well, I know when I'm beat," he said finally. "Gimme back my pin, then, little Miss Sharp and Blunt, and we'll call it square."

"What? This?" Claire removed the garnet star and threw it at his feet. "I was never so glad to be rid of anything in my life."

"I'm his widow," the girl said.

The policeman smiled.

"It's true."

He shook his head and laughed out loud. He took off his cap and wiped his face with his handkerchief. "Married, is it?" he said.

"Yes."

"To the old man in the moon?"

She nodded, grinning.

"I don't believe it," he said.

"There's all kinds of marriages. There's all kinds of love."

"I guess you'd know about that," the policeman said.

In fact, there *had* been a wedding, down at Dugan's saloon. The girl described it in detail. Moon was drunk, talking about a government pension, and, on the spur of the moment, it seemed to her, decided that he would endow her with all of his worldly possessions—a footlocker, a few books and papers in a green carpetbag, the morocco book, which Moon first told her he had found at the fairgrounds and later said had been given to him by an old friend and mentor.

She didn't know the word, and Moon explained it: "Kind of a teacher."

"Like you."

A crowd of down-and-outers looked on, waiting for the free drinks, and a bar girl they knew acted as bridesmaid, carrying a wilted bouquet of roses. Music from the professor's piano, Moon's favorite, "After the Ball," and a wedding feast from the skimpy free lunch counter. Moon slipped the horseshoe nail ring on her finger and kissed her on the forehead.

"My girl," he said. "You saved my life."

It was a pretty good joke, taken all in all, and worth a round on the house, but Moon went solemn. "This is kind of like a trick we're playing on Uncle Sam." He took her hand, she remembered, and rubbed his cheek across the sharp, white knuckles. "But believe me, I do love you, girl."

"I didn't mean what I said just now," the policeman said. "About love."

"Sure you did."

"I'm sorry," he said. "Truly."

"There's love of country," the girl said. "There's your kind of love—which is just sex, and not very entertaining either, I might add, for a girl." She blinked back tears. "There's the love of a mother for her child."

"Don't cry, I said."

She shook him off. "And then there's Moon's kind."

.   .   .

164

The wind ruffled the corn. A nighthawk cruised along the fenceline. Win sat with his back against the stone. *My father's business.* The letter Olsen had shown him bore a New York City postmark. No return address. Was Moon still alive? Had he ever remarried? If so, were there other Moons, brothers, sisters, someone to share the burden, or was he, Winslow Homer, Moon's only descendant? It made him feel lonesome, imagining the various ways Moon's life might have gone. For all he knew, his father's bones lay moldering in an unmarked grave, some potter's field, and here he was, the man's firstborn and possibly only son, resting his worthless carcass against his stone.

Had Moon ever thought about him, wondered how he turned out? Sometimes Win could almost feel his father at his back, a warmth barely grazing his shoulders that disappeared when he turned. Had Moon ever wanted to come home?

In time, the elements would batter through Moon's coffin. Water and worms and mud, a primal ooze would melt old Moon to muck and separate his bones, and one fine day a flood would come along and redistribute him. What would love or the lack of it mean then?

Win stood up and stretched, leaned on the stone, his wrists crossed lightly over the limestone pages. He stared out into the darkness, taking stock. He felt small and spiteful, sad, abandoned. He did not generate the kind of love that would anchor a man, apparently, and call out the father in him. Nor was he likely to turn out to be the hero his father was. Delmar's example was bogus, of course. He wasn't going anywhere, but that wasn't the point. Delmar had style. Win was ordinary, backward, dull, lacking his father's spirit of adventure.

Win paced the fenceline, trailing a stick along the wire, and the rows of corn seemed to open just for a moment as he passed — a glimpse of order — then closed again in confusion as he walked on.

Love.

Indifference.

Love.

At least his father had done something with his life, traveled to the fair, then clear to Alaska. Met folks, Win imagined, seen things, worked at all kinds of jobs. And he couldn't help thinking that Moon had probably faltered, too, taken a wrong turn, morally, now and then. Sure, he had lost himself in various vices. Win didn't let himself speculate too extensively, but, say, women. Moon might have dallied. He certainly drank. But wasn't that all just another part of the journey, grist for the mill, and wasn't it possible—certain, in fact—that Moon had found a higher innocence? After all, as Pastor said, there is no atonement without sin.

The morning after the wedding, Moon soaked a handkerchief in cold water and wrapped it around his head. It didn't do much to take away the pain.

Mary was still asleep, beautiful, blameless—at least, the way Moon saw it—and deserving. She was owed. He'd have to go down to Washington, find the pension bureau, and enter her name—when his headache let up—but first things first.

He tore a sheet off a tablet of paper, adjusted his elbows on the table, and wet the carpenter's pencil with his tongue.

July 7, 1914
Olsen Monuments
Winterset, Iowa

Dear Sir,

Enclosed please find crude Rendering of my Gravestone as I wish it carved. Height is to be three & one half feet approximate, with Width of Book no less than twenty inches, 22 to 24 preferred. Iowa Limestone is specified. As to ornamentation, Calla lilies, three, no more nor less, positioned so as to form a triangular pattern at the Base of what you are to simulate as a Tree Stump, oak. Deposit and delivery instructions enclosed. No Inscription required.

Your Obedient Servant,
James R. Moon

. . .

The little man was late for the meeting. "Sorry," he said. "Personal bidness. Lady friend of mine." He nodded to some of the men he knew and wiggled into a seat next to Billy Barnes.

"You shouldn't have come here," Barnes said. "This is a strategy meeting. Pullman workers only. We got to be careful."

"I wouldn't miss this meeting for the world."

Inside the hall, the little man's presence created quite a stir.

"I'm a reporter," he told the workers. "Out-of-town paper."

"Like hell."

"You're a spy," another man said. "You're making up the blacklist for the foreman."

"Gentlemen." Nick stood up. He looked around the room at each man in turn. "Now, you all know me, though you may not remember the exact circumstances of our first encounters, and you know me to be your friend and trusted confidant."

"Pullman's got 'friends' too!"

"Throw him out!"

"Goddamned spy!"

"Gentlemen, gentlemen," Nick said, "there's your spy." He whirled around and pointed to a window where one red-rimmed, startled eye was looking in.

"Get him!"

The eye blinked, then disappeared beneath the windowsill as four or five Pullman workers barreled out the door.

"It's that lunatic!" someone shouted. "Moon."

Moon took off. Pullman workers, a dozen or more, were pouring out the doorway. "Get him," they shouted. "He's running down Kensington!"

The workers gave chase. But Moon, the old sprinter, long-legged and sinewy, pumped ahead of them, head high, skinny arms churning. He gained an advantage of forty, fifty yards, and when his chance came, ducked behind some trees and was lost in the night.

The workers returned to the meeting exhausted.

"Moon," they grumbled. "Better not show his face around here again."

The meeting reconvened, and Nick was given permission to stay.

"You ain't got a vote, though," someone told him.

"That suits me right down to the ground."

Nick took a seat in the back of the room. The men were tired and angry. Bitter arguments ran back and forth, grievances months old were aired: how the children of Pullman Town had trooped to the carpentry shop all winter, begging for scrap lumber, anything that would burn, how wages were cut and rents held firm.

One or two spoke of a grudging admiration for George Pullman, a man of genius. Few men could do what he had done.

"Not relevant," someone said. "Call for the question."

"Second," the little man cried.

"Hush up!"

"Strike!"

"I'm telling you—"

"Call the question! I got places to go and people to see."

One man, a skilled mechanic, told how he had worked for twelve ten-hour days and brought home only five dollars and seven cents. Another waved a check made out for two cents, all that was left after his rent was deducted from his pay.

A thin, pale man arose in the back of the hall. "My check was forty-seven cents," he said. "They asked me, did I want to *apply* that to the rent I owed. I told 'em, 'If Mr. Pullman needs that forty-seven cents worse than I do, let him have it!'"

Sane, low-keyed arguments were tossed aside in the wake of what was now a growing panic, a rush to action, any action. Most of the men were months behind in their payments.

"Lots of despair floating around," Nick whispered to Barnes. "The time is ripe."

The sky was empty. Morning. The air was still. Sound carried for miles, and Moon, up on the ladder, working, stopped to listen: the cries of a native people betrayed, the keening of animals, rifle fire and oil wells churning, the bite of an ax, clear-cutting, relentless, until there was nothing left but a scatter of stumps.

The passenger pigeon was gone, the buffalo. The rivers had slowed, darkened with silt. Moon felt the earth give way. No growback now, but constant erosion, greed, conquest, heedless consumption with no replenishing.

And something else. It pulled him down from the ladder. The chance for a simple happiness lost.

Turning east, Moon, far gone now, saw a great mechanical hawk, a yellow smoke, a horseless carriage, armed for destruction, the wheels like two iron treadmills. Coxey's Army had fallen apart. The man himself, the old theosophist, arrested for walking on the grass in Washington, D.C. Nation rose up against nation. Money, money and dominance. Far in the distance, he heard the guns of war.

Moon paced the shoreline and wandered in and out of the crumbling buildings. White-veneered promises, dying faster than he could hope to rebuild them. Ghosts and mocking half-formed visions slipped in and out of the shadows. A phantom gondola drifted on the lagoon. Had she really been there, Mae, at the brothel? No. Impossible. Moon didn't believe it.

Visions of a son who didn't know him. A good, loving wife, forfeited. He had failed them, and what he felt for Claire, he realized now, was nothing more than a desperate need to love. She was beyond him anyway, the future, a modern girl, and though Moon wished he were still young and simple enough to love her, or anyone, he knew that he did not.

"Lockout." Someone had leaked the news. A rumor ran through the plant. Management knew about the meeting—a spy, one worker said. They knew that the men were talking strike. They intended to close the shops. But the Pullman workers refused to be dismissed. One by one they shut down their machines.

"Strike!" Billy Barnes said. "Strike, by God. You should've seen them streaming through the gates." He set his coffee cup down on the kitchen table. "Walked right out. Cora—" his eyes glistened— "we was men."

Standing behind her husband's chair, Cora put her hands on Billy's shoulders, rubbed her cheek against his hair.

"And when the embroidery girls come out, every man of us cheered."

Claire reached across the table and took her brother's hand. "Solidarity," she said.

"Solidarity, girl."

Moon tossed in his sleep. He woke in terror. A thick, fetid smoke was filling the room.

He jumped up. The window was open. "Mary!"

"What is it?"

"Cannon fire," he said.

She sat up and rubbed her eyes.

"Get up," he told her. "Gather the books."

She rose and pulled on her wrapper, joined Moon at the window.

"There," he said.

She looked where he pointed. "I don't see anything."

"There," he said. "Right down there."

Three men—Moon saw them clearly—the man in the woods, the man on the ridge, the boy, all back in service—moved in procession along the sidewalk, hand to shoulder, victims of mustard gas. Their eyes were swathed in filthy white bandages. "See?" The blind leading the blind. Farther up and across the street, the boy from the graveyard, grinning, leaned against a lamppost, truly an angel now, the perfect wound from Moon's Enfield centered in his pale forehead.

"Oh, Christ," Moon said.

"Take it easy."

Then the guns went off—cannon and small arms fire, the big Krupp gun—and the sky lit up.

"No!"

"Settle down, old man."

"Where's my boy? Winslow!"

Moon rushed past her, pulled on his trousers and grabbed his coat. He ran out the door and down the hall to the staircase, where, he hollered back to her, yellow smoke had nestled at the landing.

"Stay where you are," he said.

Moon covered his mouth with a handkerchief and started down.

There was no one in the lobby when Moon stumbled out of the stairwell. The girl had not followed. He stepped outside. The moon was out and the streets glowed as though they were blanched in lime-light. Horrible shadows. Moon looked around. The twisted bodies of young men lay in the gutters, the dark, bloated bodies of dead horses. The sweet rot of death was everywhere.

Moon started walking, keeping his head down, afraid to run. At the corner, a corpse, the legs shattered, sat like a drunkard slumped in a doorway. His gory head, split open, tilted sideways, and his tin dish hat was turned upside down in his lap like a beggar's bowl.

"What's happened?" Moon said. "Where's my boy?"

The body grinned and said nothing.

Sullivan! Moon backed away. Patch Sullivan would have some answers. Moon turned and ran south, took a corner, lost his way and found it again, running on instinct, threading through the dark streets to Sullivan's dark subterranean office.

Patch, wrapped in a horse blanket, was asleep on a flattened cardboard box. His plug hat was pulled down over his eyes.

"Patch."

Moon kicked the sole of his boot, and Sullivan sprang up, fists ready. "What the hell?"

"War." Moon grabbed him by the collar and hauled him up the stairs. "Help me find my boy."

The street was empty, quiet. The first pink light of dawn seeped over the rooftops. A window shade went up, and Moon heard the wheels of an early delivery cart, the jingle of harness. He blinked his one good eye. It seemed to him as though the smell of gunpowder hung in the air.

"What you got to show me," Patch said, yawning.

Moon was bewildered. "Winslow."

"You need a drink."

The American Railway Union was meeting in Chicago, and the Pullman strikers had asked to address the convention. If they all stood together, the strikers argued—railroad workers and Pullman factory hands—George Pullman could be made to see reason. They weren't fighting for themselves alone, they said, but for all workers. They asked the union president, Eugene Debs, to support a boycott.

Debs was hesitant. The union was green, and this would be a long and bitter struggle, nationwide, involving thousands of workers. Could they win? Only Pullman could resolve the issues without the risk of violence, but he was not willing to listen. In a last-ditch effort at negotiation, yet another workers' committee offered to meet with Pullman management. This time, however, the offer was refused.

"Well, that's the straw that broke the camel's back," the little man said.

With all means of arbitration exhausted, the railroad union voted to support the Pullman strikers and instructed its members—a hundred and fifty thousand nationwide—to refuse to handle trains with Pullman cars. On June 26 a crowd of strikers stopped the trains at Grand Crossing in South Chicago, and two days later a mail train was halted at Cairo. Riots broke out at Blue Island. Sympathy strikes erupted in twenty-three states.

"Folks running out of milk and meat. Cotton and coal, buttons and buggy whips. Commerce ground to a total standstill, U.S. mail piling up. My, my." The little man sighed. "Appears to me the system's breaking down."

Billy Barnes scowled over his breakfast. "People got a right to protect their jobs."

"Rights? Hell's fire," the little man said.

"Whose side are you on, anyway?" Moon asked him.

"Moonie, you don't have a clue what this strike is about. Up on that ladder, mooning."

"I'm rebuilding the city."

"And where's George Pullman?" Claire was furious. "Fled. That's what the people are saying. Left the city. *Vacationing* at some swanky seaside resort."

"Says here," the little man said, reading the morning paper, "that the General Managers Association, 'a leading group of railroad entre-manurers,' has requested an injunction to protect our vital rail transportation. And has asked for the aid of the U.S. marshal to enforce it."

"Surely it won't come to that," Claire said.

The little man slapped the paper down on the table. "Federal troops on the way from Fort Sheridan. Soldiers! Ain't that a kick in the kimono?"

"I understand they might camp right here in Pullman," Cora said. "On the lawn of the Hotel Florence."

"Sure." The little man dunked his toast in his coffee. "President Cleveland says we gotta protect our national interests."

"Well, I think it's awful."

"No, they got a right. Chicago's the hub, the core. Labyrinth of tracks connecting, running out ever which way. The heart of the country."

"Still."

"Chicago Northwestern, Burlington, C & O, Rock Island Line. Hauling, moving. Lumber and grain, hogs and cattle. Commerce. In she comes and out she goes."

"This is supposed to be a government of the people," Moon said, "*by* the people."

"Please," Cora said. "Mr. Moon, they're looking for you. The strikers think—"

"Debs!" Nick said. "President of the union!" He leaned across the table toward Barnes, trying to bait him. "Hell, the man had ought to be in jail."

"They think I'm a spy for Pullman," Moon told Cora. "Me. Jim Moon. Why, I'm a working man."

"We're going to have to ask you to leave. I'm sorry," she said. "But we have a child to think about."

The boss patted his lips with a linen table napkin. "Excellent, as always," he told the housemaid. She blushed a little, clearing the breakfast dishes.

The boss rose from his seat. He took his stick from the stand in the hallway and kissed his wife on the cheek. The door was held for him by a colored man. He walked out into the morning air untroubled. The sea, he had always found, had a wonderfully calming effect, not that the boss was worried. The sun was shining, and the sand was a warm and tasteful yellow-beige.

A few yards ahead, a little man sat on a rock, watching the sea. His tattered coat fluttered in the breeze. A derby hat lay on the rock beside him, anchored by a slender bamboo cane. The boss, strolling toward that very rock, the vantage point from which he daily observed the tides, was somewhat annoyed. More and more of this sort invaded the seashore every day, dragging their snot-nosed children along, carrying picnic baskets. They camped like gypsies in canvas tents, eating cold fried chicken with their fingers, wading in the surf, the women lifting their gingham skirts above the ankles, some of them, and the men forever throwing sticks for their mongrel dogs to fetch. The boss's wife, renowned for her vivaciousness, sometimes struck up conversations with these outsiders, but the boss himself remained aloof, as befitted a man of his lofty station.

When the boss passed the rock, the little man spoke. "Long time, no see."

The boss stopped, turned. "Do I know you?"

The little man just smiled.

"I'm afraid I don't . . ." The boss hesitated.

"Coming back to you?"

The boss's face changed. "I remember you now. Worker, weren't you? Salesman?"

"You got me."

"I know my men."

The boss looked out to sea, which was pale turquoise beneath an empty sky. Low breakers whispered at his feet.

"You're a gent," the little man said. "I seen your house on Prairie Avenue—just from the outside, of course."

"Chicago?"

The little man nodded.

"When were you there last?"

"Pardon?"

"Chicago, Chicago, man. When were you there?"

"Few days ago."

"What's the news?"

The little man slid off the rock and started to leave.

"Wait a minute, wait."

He walked away.

"I said wait!"

The little man turned. "Yes?"

"What's the news in Chicago? What do they say?"

"Chicago, Illinois?"

The boss's temper flared. "Sir."

The little man spat on the sand. "They say the rights of property are at war with the rights of man," he said. "They say that one law for the rich and another for the poor is a denial of liberty." He spat again.

The boss straightened his back, pulled at the wide lapels of his cashmere coat. "Do you know who I am?"

"Do you?"

"Don't trifle with me, sir. I warn you."

"Nor you with me."

The little man turned and walked away. The boss hurried after him. "And the man, Pullman?"

"Pardon?"

"What do they say of him?"

"No man envies his position."

The boss touched the little man's sleeve. "Please," he said. His eyes were pale, his skin was white. Against the empty landscape he seemed emptied out himself.

"Arrogance is mostly what he's charged with. But arrogance ain't a hanging crime. Not here. Hell, it's America. I seen your houses," the little man said. "You boys got reasons for arrogance."

"And Pullman?"

"The town?"

The boss nodded.

"They say that town is un-American."

The boss drew back. A sudden and total change came over his face. What had been sad bewilderment became, in an instant, outrage, a monstrous anger.

"Un-American?" he said.

"Feudal."

"Why, Pullman built a city. He gave them every comfort. There is running water, sir, in every flat at Pullman. Nearly so. Light. My God, there are water closets!"

"And a library," the little man added.

"Yes! Yes, there *is* a library. And at a very modest charge, too."

The little man shook his head sadly. "Ingrates!" he said. "Ever last one of them."

The policeman leaned against the door, listening to the girl's story. "So you married this old rummy."

"He stopped drinking after the wedding," she said. "Nothing but black coffee with plenty of sugar."

"Marriage sobers a man."

She ran her hands over Moon's uniform.

"Where'd you honeymoon, then?" the policeman said.

"Camden, New Jersey."

"Hell of a spot. What's wrong with Niagara?"

"Moon had business."

"When was this?"

"About a month ago."

The girl was telling the truth as far as he could tell. "Consummated?"

"What's that?"

"Show me some paper and I'll believe you," he said.

Camden, New Jersey, 1914, summer. A saloon.

"I'm looking for a man," Moon said.

"Ain't we all?"

"No, I mean a house, where a man used to live, a poet. I guess maybe I'm looking for a grave."

The woman behind the bar was almost as tall as Moon. She had coal-black hair and green eyes.

"Don't I know you from somewhere?" Moon said.

"Drink or move on." The woman jerked her thumb toward the door.

"I *do* know you."

"Hey, Roy!" the woman called over her shoulder.

"No, wait."

A burly bouncer emerged from behind a velvet curtain and grabbed Moon by the seat of the pants and the collar. He lifted Moon like a suitcase and heaved him through the swinging doors.

"Go west, old man, and stay the hell out of here."

Moon landed face down and lay in the muck for a moment thinking it over. The girl, Mary, watched him from the carriage. It was pleasant muck, a mixture of beer and mud and horse manure, and smelled like the Cedar River of Moon's beginning. Snatches of poetry came to his mind, forgotten songs and stories.

The barmaid stepped outside and leaned over Moon. A bluebird on the wing was tattooed on her plump white calf. She whispered something.

"What?" It sounded like *minstrelsy, mystery.*

"What?" Moon said. He cupped his hand to his ear.

Trickery? Was that it? "Say again."

"Mickle Street."

· · ·

The girl produced a receipt from a boarding house in Camden, New Jersey, a bill of fare. "We was there for two nights."

The policeman scanned them and tossed them back on the table. "Too bad," he said. "I was fixing to ask for your hand myself."

The girl looked up. How many men had there been, pretending love or even just lust? Little Tommy Keil, he was the first one, Dutch Meyers, him with his checkered suit and his fancy diamond stickpin. Dickie Kerr, Bryce McKinney.

"Course you know I'm teasing," he said.

"Sure." The girl glanced away. "I know."

Mickle Street was quiet, tree-lined, sour with the smell of nearby factories. An old man sat on a stoop reading the paper. An ice wagon stood at the curb. Nearby the bell of the Methodist church tolled the hour. It was three in the afternoon. Moon approached a woman hanging out wash on a clothesline.

"Who?" she said.

"Walt Whitman."

She hauled a pair of long johns out of her laundry basket and shook them out in the sun. "You say he lived next door?"

Moon nodded.

"When was that?"

"Few years back."

She talked through a mouth full of clothespins. "Don't remember."

Moon looked up. Whitman's house was modest. Three second-story windows, shuttered, faced north, vacant, impassive. Moon was years too late. Once, from those high windows—it would have been easy—the poet could have looked down on this bewildered disciple and blessed him.

"Seriously," the policeman said. "You and this old man." He hesitated. "Were you . . . ?"

"Friends," she said. "Companions."

The policeman brightened. "So you weren't . . ."

She shook her head.

"A marriage of convenience, then."

"I guess."

"Because . . ." The policeman paced the room. "I was wondering . . ."

Moon could not persuade the current Mickle Street owner to let him take a look at Whitman's rooms. No matter. He could imagine. Books, of course, papers, a heavy buffalo lap robe, a pier glass, stagnant water in a vase, a rocking chair, a clock. *After you have exhausted what there is,* Whitman had written, *in business, politics, conviviality, love, and so on—have found that none of these finally satisfy, or permanently wear—what remains?*

"I was wondering . . ."

"Want a rematch?"

The policeman reached out, as though to stroke her hair—so pretty, innocent, in a way. He stopped himself.

"Go ahead," the girl said. "I won't bite."

He studied her expression.

"Can't decide, can you?" she said.

He cupped her face in his hands. "You're too good for all of this, you know."

She kissed him. "What about you?"

"Me?"

She glanced around the room. "You see anybody else?"

He broke away. "I'm not good enough."

"What do you mean?" She fumbled for his hand. "Tell me."

"I don't know. The other men, they do the job easier somehow. They don't doubt."

"Maybe you're a cut above the other men," she said.

"You think so?"

"It's one way to look at things."

He checked the expression in her eyes. "Is it joking you are?"

"Ah, sure and it's no lie I'm telling you, Sean Michael."

He smiled.

"Come back inside," she said.

"Want me to read to you?"

"You're probably the best man among them," she said.

"I'd doubt that."

She handed him the morocco book. "I wouldn't."

Moon, as always, had waited until the girl was fast asleep. How beautiful she was, an unexpected last blessing, and just when he had almost given up hope.

He was calm now, sane, a married man. He took the stairs, knowing them in the dark, their worn iron treads, their hollow sound. They spiraled down in a way that seemed ancient and familiar, the only pattern ever possible. Under the hotel marquee he stopped to check the time. It was midnight. A light fog obscured the tops of the buildings.

Moon had a pint of Old Crow, but he didn't stop, as he sometimes did, in the shelter of a doorway to take a drink. Instead he turned south, quickened his step. The streets ran like dark streams to the river, which was not a river at all but salt water, turbulent, swift, all the way north to Hell Gate.

Moon turned up his collar, ignoring the night people, keeping private, dodging the law, the boys from Jersey. Near the water the fog deepened. At the Brooklyn Bridge it had seeped in under the roadbed, obscuring the pilings until the whole vast structure seemed to float. Moon crossed to midpoint, happy in the familiar glimmer of lights, the Gothic arches, the delicate, almost imperceptible sway. A ferryboat passed underneath him—a ghostly twinkle of lights, just the faintest outline of the hull. The bridge seemed suspended from nothing to nothing, from past to future in perfect balance, stone and steel. A motorcar came out of the fog, the headlights cutting through Moon's reverie and rushing on. Moon spit over the side of the bridge for luck.

A long drop. Moon reconsidered. He didn't want any pain.

Why not step off a ferry instead, a quick transition? After all, he had nothing left to prove. Sheltered, shadowed, under the roof of the iron cage. At the midpoint where the roadbed lifted—yes, he decided, where the twin curves of the steel ropes met.

Win stood at the stone pulpit. "Oh, heavenly Father," he intoned. He had gotten good at mimicking Pastor Rayburn's silky, hollow voice. "We are gathered here . . ."

For what? Win sat down and crossed his legs, Indian style, thinking. What *were* people here for anyway, bunched together, frightened, bored, chewing their toast in the morning and reading the paper while the rest of the world burned. Marrying people they didn't love and then proceeding to breed a bunch of . . .

Just tell the truth.

Sometimes, in the parlor with the lights turned low, Caroline let him put his arm up over the back of the settee behind her shoulders and kiss her on the lips, and that was all right. He felt pretty sure then that he wanted to marry this plain, sensible girl and settle down, even raise a little Moon or two, although the prospect of fatherhood unnerved him. That's what people do, Caroline said.

In all the time that Win was growing up, his father had written him only one letter. It came from Skagway, Alaska, when Win was five, a long harangue on life and love, a treatise, a memoir, a cri de coeur in which Jim Moon confessed to various crimes, among them murder, but failed to specify the circumstances. In search of a pure whiteness, perhaps—who knew Moon's motivation by then—solitude, peace, a savage existence. In search of gold, Win decided finally. The easiest answer.

Of course, Mrs. Ross, Win's stepmother, had read him only brief selections, editing freely and recasting certain unacceptable sentiments. "An unwanted intrusion into the precarious life of a wronged, innocent boy"—that was how Mother Ross regarded the letter. She put it aside in a hatbox with some of Mae Moon's things, and Win read the full, uncensored version only many years later, after Mrs. Ross had passed away.

It explained almost nothing. In fact, it was nearly incoherent, but Moon had enclosed the lyrics of a song, an old one, sung by the forty-niners. He liked the tune, he had written Win, a minstrel air, and some of the lyrics seemed particularly apt:

> When I left the States for gold
> Everything I had I sold;
> A stove and bed, a fat old sow,
> Sixteen chickens and a cow.
>
> On I traveled through the pines,
> At last I found the northern mines;
> I stole a dog, got whipt like hell,
> Then away I went to Marysville.
>
> I mined awhile, got lean and lank,
> And lastly stole a monte-bank;
> West to the city, got a gambler's name
> And lost my bank at the thimble game.
>
> When the elephant I had seen,
> I'm damned if I thought I was green;
> But others say, both night and morn,
> They saw him coming 'round the Horn.

Lately Win had begun to carry the letter with him. Out in Seymour's field he took it out of his pocket and read it again. He leaned against the stone and sang softly, making up the tune. They saw him coming. Green. Like Win himself, maybe. Sure. Old Moon was a boy once, too—not then, not in Alaska, of course, but he remembered. Got duped, apparently. Was it some sort of message? Pastor said that, whenever you played the fool, it was always better to tell the joke on yourself first. That way you could take the sting out of the ribbing folks were bound to give you. The stone, for instance.

He stood up and looked at the monument critically. It *was* sort of funny. The ivy curling like some flirty girl batting her eyelashes, the calla lilies all stiff and proud. A monstrosity, Caroline called it. Win was always the last one to get the joke.

He ran his hand again over the pages. The stone tickled his palm and made him smile. Tenderly, he caressed the upper right corner, chipped off at a sharp angle by one of Caroline's sledgehammer attacks. A shame because it was beautiful, too. Serious and silly harnessed together, like a bay and a dappled gray horse, pulling the same wagon.

"Oh, heavenly Father . . . Oh, Father." Win smiled. "What is this thing?"

The men at the White City huddled around the fire.

"Socialism now," somebody said. "You watch that Debs."

"I have seen, already, this," one immigrant said, "when the army comes."

"It's a twisted fate and no lie," a young Irishman told his companion. "Didn't we come over here for to get free of the landlords? And aren't they lying and thieving, the bastards, in every place in the world?"

"They won't send troops to the city," Moon said. "You don't think they'll come here."

"No, general," Nick said. "I have doubled the guards at the gate." He saluted.

"You think I'm fooling," Moon said.

"I think you are a fool."

Moon had been one of the boys earlier, roaming the Rock Island tracks. Two or three got to rocking an empty freight car—it wasn't hard. A good push and over it went. Simple as pie. The mob cheered. Moon took another drink. His heart was racing. Switches were thrown. The boys began to pelt the cars with stones.

Somebody sidled up to Moon and offered him five dollars to torch a boxcar. Conflagration. Moon, drunk and gullible, liked the old notion of a fire sweeping clean. "Help the cause," the fellow told him. "Show those bosses who's really the boss."

Idealists are the best pawns. The true believers. An excess of love bewilders them. They are so eager. Empty and sidetracked, the car went up like kindling, chattering nonsense. Moon was elated.

Rioting—and this was one of many things that Moon never understood—gave the bosses just what they needed to justify the use of federal troops.

"Nice work," the fellow said. He handed Moon a five. One car ignited the next, a chain of fire sweeping down the tracks. The dry, brittle wood sent up an exaltation of sparks.

"Jim?"

The voice came out of the darkened doorway. Moon would have known it anywhere.

"I have to talk to you," she said.

Moon took a quick nip from the bottle. *Mae.* "Have you seen the city? Gosh, I been hoping you'd come. I didn't want you to miss it. Course, she's a little the worse for wear now, but—"

"Jim, listen."

"I'm rebuilding. It'll be just like it was."

She closed her eyes, opened them, looked at Moon as though she were seeing him now for the first time.

"Come on back outside." Moon reached for her hand. "The stars are out."

"I have something to tell you," she said. "It's important."

"Hush." Moon placed a wet, drunken kiss on her face. "You're here. Everything's all right now."

He led her to the Grand Basin. "Ain't this something?" he said. "Just like I dreamed it."

The White City was awash in moonlight, shimmering under a clear cobalt sky. Moon's ladder was propped against the side of the building, and a section of the east wall was newly coated with staff. The lake whispered at the shoreline, and they could hear the voices of homeless men camped along the basin. Their fires flickered in the night.

"It is beautiful," she said.

"The work's going real good."

She kissed him. She stroked his hair. "My very dear lunatic."

She took his hand and eased it along her waistline. Her blue cotton dress pulled tight at the seams. "I'm with child."

Moon stepped back and tried to focus.

"They brought in this . . . doctor," she said. "They wanted to kill my baby, the woman there and a man named Nick, but I wouldn't let them."

Moon tried to take her in his arms, but she broke away.

"There were so many, Jim. Night after night. Didn't you see me? Why didn't you come back?"

THE MOROCCO BOOK:

Thing is, she was useless to me. Might as well deliver her back to Moon. The boys in the ward ain't fussy, but a pregnant gal . . . Offends the sensibilities and difficult to achieve the proper angle. Gave her a five and flipped her the garnet pin. A token, a farewell gift, if you get my drift.

Moon rushed back inside and grabbed the little man by the collar. "I'll kill you!"

The little man broke away. He ran down the Court of Honor, with Moon right behind him. They circled the basin, Moon losing ground. From time to time the little man looked over his shoulder and grinned.

Moon was winded. He sat down on an iron bench to rest.

"You gettin' old," Nick said. "I seen the time Jim Moon could not be beat in a foot race."

Moon leaned his elbows on his knees, trying to catch his breath. "Why? Why did you do it?" he said. "You didn't have to."

"Oh, but I did. It was there to be done. Such easy pickings. If I hadn't done it, another man would have. Then where'd I be? Why, second in line, cornpone. And Nickels ain't a second-place kind of man."

"You ain't a man at all," Moon said. "You're some kind of contagion."

"You're getting warmer."

"What you intend to do about it?" Moon said.

"What's that?"

"My wife."

"Hadn't thought much about it," the little man said. "Really ain't my problem, is it?"

"I'd say it is."

Nick sat down on the bench beside Moon. "Well, there's this gypsy gal I know. She got some tricks."

"What are you talking about?"

"You're a farm boy. You know how it's done. All it takes is a sharp stick."

Jim Moon jumped up. "I'll, by God, throttle you." He grabbed the little man by the throat and pulled him to his feet, pressing his thumbs in hard. He would have killed him if he hadn't looked into his eyes.

"Can't do it, can you?" Nick said.

Moon relaxed his grip.

"Recognize me?"

Moon denied it.

"Sure."

THE MOROCCO BOOK:

So they're watching Blue Island, watching Pullman, feds looking out for them agitators causing all the trouble, spiking switches, stopping trains. Old Dictator Debs gonna bring the country down, they say, social disorder abroad in the land. My, my, class conflict. Ain't it awful? All them bohunks, wops, polacks, micks (the worst), stirring them up, and then the night of July Five, a fire of "unknown origins"—haw, haw—breaks out down in them exposition buildings, the White City.

Jackson Park ablazing.

At last.

As you know, I am something of a connoisseur of fire.

.   .   .

The little man, free of Moon's grasp, stepped back. He seemed taller now, more menacing. "You just what I thought you were," he said.

Moon grabbed a firebrand and swung it. The little man ducked and grabbed hold of the shaft. "Know me now?"

Moon backed away.

The little man waved the torch. "Come on, boys. Let's see some fun."

The men stirred and stood up, looking for action.

"Ain't you tired of wanting? Don't you hate the dream?"

"Damn right!" somebody said.

"Then follow me."

The little man threw the torch in the air. It sailed like a javelin. One of the buildings ignited. The mob was running.

"Get that spy!" The little man pointed at Moon. "That scab, that anarchist." The men turned on Moon.

Another building began to glow, then burst into flame. Staff burned like tinder, showering sparks. The crowd broke apart in confusion, and Moon saw the little man everywhere.

"It was too much for you, Moon," he said. "Finally found paradise, and what'd you do?"

The Manufactures Building was lost in flames. Fire licked the length of the roofline and played in and out of the windows. The lath blackened and fell away, leaving the iron skeleton exposed.

The little man stood in the glare of the flames, holding Mae.

"Did you live? Moon? Did you take this woman here in your arms?"

THE MOROCCO BOOK:

So, this Mae, she breaks loose, runs back, back, back, into a burning building—can you see it? Lost in smoke and darkness, crazy, crying out for Moon. That's theater, folks.

And he saves her, o' course. Old Hero Moon. In a manner of

speaking. Just at the fateful juncture. Hauls her out like a sack of potatoes. No finesse, but it's the thought that counts.

I stroll in a little bit later. Curious, you know, to see the end.

Over Moon's head, the building started to sway. The largest building ever constructed by man. Iron beams fell, not separately, but in one final fiery collapse. And Moon stepped back, steps back, and the air, when he takes it in, the air is hot and dark. The air is empty, full of death. It explodes inside his chest.

"Burned up," the girl said.

"Looks like."

"That was my mother, then, this Mae Moon."

"Must have been."

It took her a while to understand. "He saved her and took off."

"They were after him, I guess."

She wiped her eyes on her sleeve. "No wonder Moon didn't want me to know."

The policeman sat on the bed beside her, holding her hand.

"Burned up," she said. "Then how . . ."

THE MOROCCO BOOK:

A biscuit in the oven. Haw, haw. Face blistered up, fingers melted together. Old Moon caught fire himself, dragging her out. That was me that doused him.

"They took her to Cook County," Michael said. "The first doctor wouldn't even agree to work on her, said she was too far gone, but the book says there was a nun assisting. A Sister Mary Theresa." He stroked her hair. "You know us Catholics."

"And I was . . ."

Curled up in her belly, floating in darkness.

"So . . ."

A split of light, a rush of cold, hands reaching in, lifted, seeing the light for the first time through bloody water.

Whitman's tomb was a stone cottage. Massachusetts granite, a wrought-iron gate.

> You will hardly know who I am or what I mean,
> But I shall be good health to you nevertheless,
> And filter and fibre your blood.
>
> Failing to fetch me at first keep encouraged,
> Missing me one place search another,
> I stop somewhere waiting for you.

Moon tried to peer into the gloom. Weak, watery light on white marble, a shadow, a scurry along the floor. Moon inhaled the savory dust of death. Whitman's skull, empty in its crypt, was only a place for the insects to do their work now, only a shell, but Moon didn't know that and whispered into the darkness: "What remains?"

"You all right?" the policeman said.

The girl nodded.

"Sure?"

"Sure," she said.

She stood up and walked to the door, fished in Moon's coat pockets and pulled out a bundle of crumpled papers. "You might as well have these," she said. "That's everything."

A few notes in Moon's hand, an unposted letter to his son, a list of architects, a sepia-tinted picture of Moon against a background of snow, a half-dozen stock certificates for something called the Ala-moon Mining Company in Dawson City, Alaska. "Worthless," she said.

The girl found Moon's army discharge papers. "I was hoping I might get a pension or something."

"What about his son, this Winslow fellow?"

"He'll make out."

He stared at her.

"I told you I was his widow," she said. "You could just fill in my name."

"That wouldn't be quite honest, now would it?"

He smiled at her and she smiled back. "Guess not. We weren't really married."

Michael pulled out his pipe and began to fill it.

"What happens now?" she said.

"We'll put him under—the heat and all. See if we can track down his people from these."

"You gonna send him back to Iowa?" she said.

"All depends. If they send the money."

She stroked the fabric of Moon's coat. "He was a good old boy," she said. "My darling."

Winslow leaned on Moon's stone, meditating on how, if some flimsy pine coffin did, in fact, contain old Moon and if, as is the nature of destruction and rebirth, it were to burst open, Moon would flow like a river and merge with the land. It was not a terrible thing to be dead. It was only a stop, one of many, perhaps, on a long migration.

Win ran his hands over the stone, taking in its hollows and contours, sensing its heft. Who wanted a father a fella could bottle up and make a speech about? Who wanted the truth if it was only a monument? Win felt he had gotten to the bottom of things, in his own way and as far as understanding was possible, teased out the limestone mystery. The marker was useless to him now. Still, he loved it, its shape and color, the cold grain beneath his hands, and he wished he could lift it and put it whole in his pocket, carry it with him wherever it was he was going.

Suddenly he heard the sound of a young woman's laughter. Her voice was shrill, hollow, and trailing it through the corn rows, Win found Caroline reclining in the arms of Delmar Avery, who wore a natty uniform of his own devising, complete with a Sam Browne belt—a convenient handle, Winslow found, with which to wrestle the rival to his feet. Win's strength seemed to come in a rush, from resources he didn't know that he had. He felt as though, if he wanted to, he could fling Avery all the way into Missouri.

"Now, see here, Moon," Avery blustered.

"You hush." Winslow gave him a shove, and Avery sat down hard.

"Win, it isn't anything like you think," Caroline said. "Delmar and me was talking."

Win glared.

She stood up and brushed her skirt. "It's a woman's duty," she said, "to give a soldier some comfort. Besides, it ain't like you and me are engaged. Not really. And the rate you're going, we never will have enough to get married on."

Winslow felt the blood pulse in his temples.

"Winnie?"

Win's eyes glittered with rage, amusement.

"Don't lose your head now, Win."

"'The Moving Finger writes; and, having writ, moves on.'" Winslow paused for effect. "'Nor all thy piety nor wit,'" he declared solemnly, "'shall lure it back to cancel half a line; nor all thy tears wash out a word of it.'"

Caroline stared.

"Omar Khayyám," he said.

And Moon came floating free, rising through the orange peels and beer bottles and cigarette butts of the river, the muck clearing temporarily as he bobbed to the surface. Shriven.

I celebrate myself and sing myself . . .

Strange to see the sun again through a wet, unblinking eye. Moon felt a little stiff. A river patrol boat crew took charge of the body, hauled Moon over the gunwale and threw a tarpaulin over his face.

"Some Bowery bum," one of them said.

Michael studied the girl. "No money," he said.

"Nope."

"I suppose you've looked everywhere."

She reached over and lifted the hem of the blanket, showing him there was nothing under the bed. She lifted the carpetbag and dumped out a cloud of dust and lint. "Nothing," she said. "Nothing there." She opened her hands and showed him her flat white palms. "Nothing." She lifted her skirt.

"All right, all right. I take your point."

She smiled.

"But listen to me." He leaned over the bed and stared hard. "Get rid of it."

"Rid of what?"

"Okay," he said. "We've come to an understanding."

The Whitman book lay on the table. He ran his fingers over the gold-stamped cover.

"You can have that if you want," she said, watching him.

He opened the book at random and scanned a page. "I'm not much of a reader."

"Might come in useful." She held her breath.

"I doubt it."

"You could use the pages to light your pipe."

He smiled. "'I bequeath myself to the dirt to grow from the grass I love,'" he read. "'If you want me again look for me under your bootsoles.'"

He closed the book and raised a heavy black brogan off the floor, bent and peered underneath it. "Nothing," he said.

September 9, 1914
Coroner's Office
City Hall
New York City, New York

To Whom It May Concern
Dear Sir,

I am much obliged for the information regarding James Ransom

Moon, late of your city. I am sure your office has done all that is proper, and I thank you for it.

My father and I have long been estranged, and though I have forgiven him with all my heart, as for removal as you have suggested, I believe it is in the best interests of all concerned that my father's remains remain where they are at present interred.

Signed,
A Dutiful and Loving Son,
W. H. Moon.

In that fall of 1914, Charles de Gaulle was wounded in combat. Young Adolf Hitler, a German private, won the Iron Cross, Second Class. At Mons, some spoke of seeing an angel holding back the German advance, a woman in the sky on a white horse. In the Battle of the Frontiers, France alone lost a hundred and forty thousand men in four days. On August 25, Louvain began to burn — the houses, the library. The German plan was sheer terror, *Schrecklichkeit*. War on civilians, the wreck of a civilization. Benito Mussolini, then a socialist, was advocating the Allied cause to the leaders of Italy, who were still neutral. "Neutrals never dominate events," he told them. "Blood alone moves the wheels of history."

Michael stood in the doorway. "So who is your father, then, if it isn't old J. R. Moon?"

The girl said nothing at first. Looking close, Michael saw a flicker in her eyes.

"It's all of you."

He backed away.

"Every one of you that took a piece." She walked to the window and stared out. "Except Jim Moon. He never."

Believe me.

Her skin was pale. Her hair seemed to glow. Michael couldn't stop staring.

"That's right, isn't it?" she said. "He never did no harm, nor wanted to."

Her eyes were as clear as rainwater, the color of prairie gentians, and she was smiling.

"Just loved her," she said, wonder in her voice. "And me. He *loved* me. Didn't he? The best he could."

Winslow was dozing on the porch swing when the dynamite went off. Not really sleeping, he came awake in time to see the sky light up over Eule Seymour's field. He was too far away to see the stone heave up and break apart, but he could imagine it rising over the cornstalks.

He rushed out to the road and ran west. From the rise near the church he saw smoke floating across the field and Caroline and Delmar Avery walking back arm in arm and whispering to each other.

"Evening, Winslow," Caroline said as they strolled past him. "You're up late."

Delmar giggled. "Thunder probably woke him up."

"Prob-ub-*lee*," she said.

Winslow raced past them and into the field. Only rubble and a muddy crater remained on the site where the preaching stone had been. Chips of limestone glowed in the moonlight, like a map of stars in the mud, and Winslow saw his direction clearly for the first time in his life. Off to the east was the bell tower and Caroline walking away with Avery. North was the road to Des Moines and the seminary. To the south, Winslow saw Eule Seymour, pulling up his suspenders as he ran and swearing loudly to whoever was there to hear him. A lot of corn had been damaged in the blast, and somebody was going to have to pay.

"There is that in Art—a Vision above fact—that makes Decisions easy," Winslow's father had written him, "directing the Mind's Eye to the obvious Good."

Winslow could not now literally take a page from his father's book, but he was able to salvage one small corner, a pyramid chip of limestone that perfectly fit in the palm of his hand. A talisman, a good-luck piece. He had it in his pocket later that same night when, carrying a few books and drawings in a satchel, he hitched a ride to the railroad depot at Creston, where he caught the midnight train headed west.

What remains? After a failure of courage, a failure of love?

The land and its population. Birds in flight, cattle, a comic grasshopper on a leaf. The roots remain, the hope in seasons. A boy and a girl.

Light and shadow remain, the shift of branches on the wind, the rivers remain, a sliver of stone. The solace of mountains, the high, wide emptiness of the west. The gracious, melancholy south. The eastern arrogance, the blue-green northlands curving in toward the pole, thinning, breaking apart, dissolving in water.

Michael hurried down the stairs. What did it matter who the old geezer was? Weren't there a dozen washed up every week?

He spun through the revolving doors and was spit out onto the pavement. He felt the heat of it through his bootsoles, an almost animal warmth. The sun was low, carving angular shadows across the street, and the buildings were caught in a pale, flat wash of gold.

Five o'clock. The factories were still throbbing. Newsboys hawked the papers, all about war. A carriage rounded the corner, the steady *pock*, *pock* of the horse's hooves like the sound of a ticking clock. The scissors sharpener came by, pushing a handcart, ringing a hollow bell. A boy on a bicycle materialized, pedaling furiously, an odd confounding of man and machine. Michael stepped aside, and the boy whizzed by on his way to the future. A drunkard, earning a meal by wearing a sandwich board, stopped to check the gutter for cigarette butts. Old men woke from dreamless afternoon naps. Women hurried home, wondering what to fix for supper. Merchants rolled up their awnings and locked their shops.

Michael settled his hat, angled it to the right. Maybe he would find a reason to go by her place again. Clean up the details. Take her to supper. Why not? Take her to the moving-picture show.

A shadow of something above him caught his eye—a bird, a leaf, a bit of paper kiting on the air. He turned and looked up. Was it leaves that were falling? Shadows, something gray, green, fluttering down. A bird's dull sheen in the waning sunlight, rain, garbage heaved from an upstairs window? He took off his cap and leaned back to look.

Paper. Spilling over his shoulders. Greenbacks. Jesus Christ, the girl was daft.

It spiraled down, money, a spill of joy, and through the gray-green snow he saw her, leaning from the window, shaking the book—something about the grass, wasn't it?—twisted inside out. Tens and twenties floated down. Holy Mother of God.

The street urchins were wise instantly, snatching it up, and even the women, well-dressed and proper, lifted their heavy skirts in order to chase it. Laughing, they fought with the children for fivers, and men wrestled the women. One of his colleagues, Mahon, happened by and tried to break it up, but there was a crowd now, pushing and shoving, a mob, a carnival.

Mahon pounded his stick on the pavement, calling for reinforcements. "Bring in the Black Maria, man," Michael said. "You won't run this lot off."

He looked up at the girl, and she was laughing.

"Not quite what I had in mind," he hollered.

Her dress was undone. Her hair was down. The button from his coat was still in her hand, or so he hoped. Christ, she was a corker.

THE MOROCCO BOOK:

See, the way I see it, I see it like George Pullman did. A man has got to take and use, and that, as the lady said, is civilization. And the worker has a choice, which is take it or leave it, which is nothing personal, which is just bidness.

A man of "imagination"—I use that term with deference but, I confess, little true understanding—is just an impediment, a monkey wrench in the great wheels of progress, and, I might add, his own worst enemy.

What was not found: Moon's leather eye patch, his souvenirs, answers, Mae Moon's grave, a letter written to Mary Grimes, washed out of Moon's pocket, which bleached white in less than a day, the ink bleeding into the river.

All goes onward and outward, nothing collapses,
And to die is different from what any one supposed, and luckier.

The strike collapsed. By mid-July the trains were running on schedule. The shops at Pullman opened again, and those who hadn't wandered away gave up their union cards and went back to work. Pullman died in 1897, five years after Walt Whitman and seventeen years before Moon. Because of the recent unpleasantness at Pullman Town, his family feared reprisals and had the casket overlaid with a layer of steel and concrete. Fortified. Like the tombs of the old pharaohs.

Prosperity returned. Robert Todd Lincoln, the president's son, was named director of the Pullman Palace Car Company. William Vanderbilt and J. P. Morgan, who had never gone to war, joined the PPCC board of directors. Debs was jailed. Clarence Darrow defended his case, and lost. Billy Barnes died in a streetcar accident in 1900. He was thirty-five. Cora lived through World War II, and Alice Barnes—called Claire—eventually got to vote. Two years after she turned down the little man, she married a young liberal named Tom Callahan, and they had a son, Robert James, who died in the Great War. Automobiles and electric light became commonplace, the airships Moon read about. In 1908, the Pullman Palace Car Company switched to an all-steel construction for its cars, which is cheaper and much safer than wood.

The photograph dated October 10, 1893—taken by Claire on the Midway's Street in Cairo—was among the various papers discovered in Moon's hotel room. In it Moon has his right hand sunk in his trouser pocket, his left elbow raised at a right angle, shoulder high. He is leaning north, precariously, leaning against nothing but ghostly space. "Me and Cornpone," someone has scribbled on the back of the picture, but the figure posed with Moon is obscure. Caught in motion, perhaps, or faded with age. The face, beneath a shadowy derby, is smoky and indistinct.

Behind them, the sun is setting—huge, theatrical. A camel passes by, for comic relief, and Moon looks left, a curious smile on his face, as though he is astonished—something has vanished. Or as though, perhaps, against all odds, he still expects something sublime to appear.